Reign of the SEVEN SPELLBLADES

VIII

Bokuto Uno

ILLUSTRATION BY
Ruria Miyuki

Yuri Leik

Nanao Hibiya

Oliver Horn

"Rule number one of fighting a powerful foe—before you strike, assume they have backup coming."

Lesedi Ingwe

"Ha-ha! Thank you, thank you. Showing up on the first day I'm around?"

Tim Linton

Pete Reston

Guy Greenwood

Katie Aalto

"Go ahead.
I'm in no mood
to be picky."

Cyrus Rivermore

"Ooh, a consolation concert? Can I make a request?"

???

CONTENTS

of the Seven Spellblades
Bokuto Uno

Reign of the SEVEN SPELLBLADES

VIII

Bokuto Uno

ILLUSTRATION BY
Ruria Miyuki

YEN
ON

New York

Reign of the Seven Spellblades, Vol. 8
Bokuto Uno

Translation by Andrew Cunningham
Cover art by Ruria Miyuki

NANATSU NO MAKEN GA SHIHAISURU Vol. 8
©Bokuto Uno 2021
Edited by Dengeki Bunko
First published in Japan in 2021 by KADOKAWA CORPORATION, Tokyo.
English translation rights arranged with KADOKAWA CORPORATION, Tokyo
through TUTTLE-MORI AGENCY, INC., Tokyo.

English translation © 2023 by Yen Press, LLC

Yen On
150 West 30th Street, 19th Floor
New York, NY 10001

Visit us at yenpress.com
facebook.com/yenpress
twitter.com/yenpress
yenpress.tumblr.com
instagram.com/yenpress

First Yen On Edition: May 2023
Edited by Yen On Editorial: Rachel Mimms
Designed by Yen Press Design: Andy Swist

Yen On is an imprint of Yen Press, LLC.
The Yen On name and logo are trademarks of Yen Press, LLC.

Library of Congress Cataloging-in-Publication Data
Names: Uno, Bokuto, author. | Miyuki, Ruria, illustrator. | Keller-Nelson, Alexander,
translator. | Cunningham, Andrew, translator.
Title: Reign of the seven spellblades / Bokuto Uno ; illustration by Ruria Miyuki ;
v. 1–3: translation by Alex Keller-Nelson ; v. 4–8: translation by Andrew Cunningham.
Other titles: Nanatsu no maken ga shihai suru. English
Description: First Yen On edition. | New York, NY : Yen On, 2020–
Identifiers: LCCN 2020041085 | ISBN 9781975317195 (v. 1 ; trade paperback) |
ISBN 9781975317201 (v. 2 ; trade paperback) | ISBN 9781975317225
(v. 3 ; trade paperback) | ISBN 9781975317249 (v. 4 ; trade paperback) |
ISBN 9781975339692 (v. 5 ; trade paperback) | ISBN 9781975339715
(v. 6 ; trade paperback) | ISBN 9781975343446 (v. 7 ; trade paperback) |
ISBN 9781975352240 (v. 8 ; trade paperback)
Subjects: CYAC: Fantasy. | Magic—Fiction. | Schools—Fiction.
Classification: LCC PZ7.1.U56 Re 2020 | DDC [Fic]—dc23
LC record available at https://lccn.loc.gov/2020041085

ISBNs: 978-1-9753-5224-0 (paperback)
978-1-9753-5225-7 (ebook)

10 9 8 7 6 5 4 3 2 1

LSC-C

Printed in the United States of America

Third-Years

Oliver Horn

The story's protagonist. Jack-of-all-trades, master of none. Swore revenge on the seven instructors who killed his mother.

Nanao Hibiya

A samurai girl from Azia. Believes that Oliver is her destined sword partner.

Katie Aalto

A girl from Farnland, a nation belonging to the Union. Has a soft spot for the civil rights of demi-humans.

Guy Greenwood

A boy from a family of magical farmers. Honest and friendly. Has a knack for magical flora.

Pete Reston

A studious boy born to nonmagicals. Capable of switching between male and female bodies.

Michela McFarlane

Eldest daughter of the prolific McFarlane family. A master of the pen and sword, she looks out for her friends.

Tullio Rossi

A lone wolf who taught himself the sword by ignoring the fundamentals. Lost to Oliver in a duel.

Yuri Leik

A transfer student. What he lacks in sense, he makes up for in boundless curiosity. Chummy with everyone.

∽ Fay Willock

∽ Joseph Albright

∽ Stacy Cornwallis

Jasmine Ames
Has distinctively long bangs. While she claims to lack confidence, her sword art skills are among the best in her year.

Rose Mistral
His every move is oddly showy, like a stage performer. Bedazzles with a blend of magic and deceit.

Richard Andrews
A proud youth from a prestigious family. Recognizes Oliver's and Nanao's talents and considers them worthy rivals.

Sixth-Years

Tim Linton
Small and cute yet short-tempered and aggressive. Known and feared as the Toxic Gasser.

Seventh-Years

Alvin Godfrey
Student council president. Nicknamed Purgatory by his peers. Boasts incredible firepower.

Lesedi Ingwe
Keeps a tight rein on Kimberly's student body as the Watch's overseer. Harsh on herself and others.

Cyrus Rivermoore
A necromancer who controls the bones of the dead. Ambushed Godfrey and stole one of his bones.

Leoncio Echevalria
Leader of the previous student council's faction. Once battled Godfrey for the presidency and received burns to the right side of his face, which he refuses to heal.

Instructors

Esmeralda
Kimberly's headmistress. Proudly stands at the apex of magical society.

Vanessa Aldiss
Magical biology instructor. Feared by her students for her wild personality.

Enrico Forghieri DECEASED
Magical engineering instructor. Prone to outrageous lessons designed to maim students.

Theodore McFarlane
Chela's father and the man who sent Nanao to Kimberly.

- Demitrio Aristides
- Frances Gilchrist
- Luther Garland
- Dustin Hedges
- Darius Grenville DECEASED

Spring, six years ago. The day of the entrance ceremony.

"Ah, so this is the famous ancient Jack."

New students streamed down Flower Road to the school building. One boy stopped along the way, gazing up at the ancient cherry tree. Any number of other students followed in his wake—hangers-on, under his thumb before they'd even arrived. Their presence, coupled with his arrogant tone, sent a message that his was a name of some repute.

"Had it failed to be in full bloom for my arrival, I was prepared to give it a good kick."

"Has it met with your approval?"

"Yes, barely. But it *has* earned a passing grade. I see no need to dirty my boots here."

Nodding at his crony's question, he continued gazing up into Jack's boughs. That is, until irritated snarls reached his ears.

"Yo, keep moving. You're blocking the path."

"Don't you see the bottleneck behind you?!"

Complaints from the crowd at his back, as to be expected—this was a one-lane road down which all new students had to proceed. Strolling leisurely while gazing at the flowers was one thing, but any break in the flow created a jam, especially with so many flunkies at the boy's side.

Except he merely snorted, hardly sparing the irritated first-years a sidelong glare.

"I could ask you the same," he said. "The path remains open. Proceed."

He glanced toward the rear of his gaggle, where a small pocket remained—just barely wide enough for someone to squeeze through.

The students arguing with him looked ready to pop a vein.

"...Unlikely as it seems, by '*path*,' you mean that sliver?"

"We gotta go single file? Everyone behind you's gotta squeeze themselves through, then?"

The scowls behind them deepened. Resolutely blocking their way, the arrogant boy had the gall to look faintly surprised.

"That is how the weak abide. A lesson you ought to have learned by now."

No remorse for his actions—rather, utter contempt for those speaking to him. That was the last straw for this crowd. Words would be useless here. Their hands reached for wands or blades.

"...Picking a fight before we're even through the gates, huh?"

"Time to smash that nose in."

They, too, were Kimberly first-years and not about to let anyone their age mock them. The boy's flunkies all braced themselves. The tension was so thick, you could cut it with a knife—but instead...

"...Augh?!"

"Eek—!"

"Wha...?"

Shrieks went up from behind. Puzzled, all turned to look—and found the crowd parting to make way for something else. Looming over the retreating crowd was the top half of a rectangular black box.

""""...Ngh...?!"""""

The parting crowd at last revealed the lower half: a boy, carrying a coffin twice his size. His feet sank into the soil with each step he took, his breathing heavy but steady, his eyes sparing not a glance for the blooms that lined the path. His stride soon took him to the factions clashing before ancient Jack the Unblooming.

"*Move.*"

The moment his voice echoed, every soul stepped aside: the boy who'd first blocked the path, his cronies, and the students who'd picked a fight with them. All here were mages, and their instincts told them loud and clear—this was not someone to trifle with.

He passed through the eye of the conflict, taking one step at a time, heedless of the first-years giving him a wide berth. A voice drifted down from the coffin on his back, the voice of a girl that only he could hear.

"Almost at the school, Cyrus. Did you say hi to the other new students? First impressions are everything!"

"I did. Lots of surprisingly pliant meat."

"Honestly, you have *got* to stop calling people '*meat*'! I've told you this over and over; you'll never make friends that way!"

Letting her lecture go in one ear and out the other, he passed through the gates, and looming ahead was the school building, his new place of learning. The edifice projected pomp and gloom in equal measure. To the boy's eyes, it reeked of death—no more and no less than his own home. He put his impressions into words.

"...Like a tomb."

Yet, a smile played on his lips. One glance had made him certain. Here, his search would not be in vain.

"It'll do. I can scavenge both meat and bones as I please."

CHAPTER 1

Planning

"Hmm-hmm. They got ye good."

"...Nn...!"

Kimberly's first-floor infirmary, the domain of the school physician, Gisela Zonneveld. A man lay on her operating table, writhing in agony—the student body president, Alvin Godfrey.

"Slipshod, Godfrey. Won't end up like this 'less ye leave yourself wide open."

"...Fair point..."

As he gasped an answer, Dr. Zonneveld roughly probed his chest cavity like a short-order cook in a greasy diner. She had a habit of making her patients feel like so much meat on a slab. Kimberly students were known for learning healing magic faster than average, mainly because nobody wanted to end up in the school infirmary.

"The flesh—well, the bone's gone, but that's nary a concern. But your ether, you cannae leave that unguarded. **Deformatio.**"

She pulled her hand, dripping with blood, out of him; the athame in her other hand was pointed at a white stone as she chanted a spell that altered it into the shape of a bone—the exact shape of the sternum Godfrey had lost.

"I'm planting a fake 'un for you. You're a regular here, boyo. Ye get my drift, yeah?"

That was a warning to brace himself. The man gritted his teeth. He'd been here several times a year, every year. He knew how this doctor worked—like how she almost never used anesthetic.

"...Any time."

So his answer was in full knowledge of that. Dr. Zonneveld grinned and took a tight grip on the fake bone.

"Good answer. Scream all ye like, but don't bite your tongue!"

She slammed the bone into the wound, and it snapped into place. A literal bone-shaking blow. Godfrey did his level best to stifle the scream trying to tear its way out of his throat.

The treatment over with, Dr. Zonneveld sat at the window, smoking. There was a knock at the door, and several students came in—at the fore, Lesedi Ingwe, a veteran member of the Watch.

"Dr. Zonneveld, how's Godfrey doing?"

The doctor didn't even turn around, just blew a puff of smoke out the window.

"...Made a new bone, slotted it in," she answered matter-of-factly through the smoke. "The ether wound is not so easily healed. Not that large a tear, so it *can* be fixed, but expect it to take two months."

Every face turned grim. With elections looming, that was far too long. Worse yet, the combat league was ongoing.

"While the ether body's damaged, ye cannae escape disruptions in mana manipulation. This fella'll be up and about in days, but in a fight, he'll be useless. Kah-ha-ha-ha! Yer up shit's creek, fraid."

"There's no way to speed it along?" Lesedi asked, ignoring the bait.

This got the doctor to spin around and point her cigarette at the Watch members.

"There is, and you know it. Get the bone back. The ether's stuck on it. If I have that, won't take me even five minutes."

Lesedi nodded. The doctor here knew no kindness, but she never once embellished a patient's condition. If she said she could fix it, she would. If she said she couldn't, she couldn't. If she said they were dead, they'd die. And thus—if she claimed she could fix Godfrey's ether in five minutes, the only option was to bring her the missing bone.

"Very well. Gimme a few days." With that, Lesedi turned on her heel and led her company out. On her way down the hall, she spat, "Urgent summons."

"…That…sure was a turnup…," Katie whispered.

The common room was abuzz with chatter about the match, including Katie, who recalled the cause of said turnup.

Across the table, Guy folded his arms, groaning. "They hauled Godfrey straight to the infirmary after the prelim. Is he gonna be okay?"

"…We can't be sure. But it's hardly a minor injury."

"If his recovery's prolonged, it'll affect the election as well as the league. I do hope I'm fretting over nothing, yet…"

Chela trailed off, taking a sip of tea. As a silence settled over them…a voice came from below.

"Um…I hate to interrupt the gloom, but…Oliver? Nanao?"

"Yes, Leik?"

"Speak, Yuri."

"Why am I being restrained?"

Oliver and Nanao were on either side of him, holding him firmly in place. He was facedown with both their hands on his shoulders.

"Because if we release you, you'll go rushing into the labyrinth," Oliver replied. "Don't be so hasty. The plan to meet Rivermoore on campus might be a bust, but I'm working on an alternative."

"Okay, I can wait. I promise! So I'd *really* appreciate you letting me go. This floor is quite hard and rather cold."

"Ah! Yuri, squirm like that and your shoulder may dislocate."

"I'm well aware of your strength, Nanao! I feel it in my creaking joints!"

Oliver ignored Yuri's protestations, his mind racing. They were waiting for the upperclassmen's move. The ambush on President Godfrey had been a shock to everyone, but that had made Cyrus Rivermoore the enemy of the Watch—the current student council. Reprisals were a given. And he planned to keep Yuri down until those plans were announced.

His prediction was proven right mere minutes later. Bird familiars came in through the window, dropping letters on the students in the room—including their table.

"Oh—!"

"What's this?"

Each student received one, and a seventh letter was left to flutter slowly down to Yuri's head. Oliver glanced around and saw Stacy and Fay opening letters of their own.

Peering at the contents, Chela frowned.

"Attendance requested by the Watch. But including third-years?"

"…We'll have to go and see what's up," said Oliver.

"Indeed! I shall haul Yuri along."

"I can walk! I have feet of my own!"

They arrived at the classroom specified and found quite a crowd already gathered. Glancing around the faces assembled, Oliver and Chela soon spotted a trend.

"…Combat-league participants?"

"Looks like we're the core, yes. I don't see Rick's team, so they didn't call in *everybody*."

"Oh, they brought you in, too, Team Horn?"

As they stepped in, a voice called out from the corner. A boy in regulation uniform, very studious-looking—it took Oliver a second, but then he placed the distinct nose.

"…Mr. Mistral. Sorry, but you gave a rather different impression during the match."

"Can't keep myself that amped up all the time, can I? I'm more the bookworm type, really."

"…Come to think of it, I *have* seen you in the library," Pete said, squinting at him.

"Mr. Reston, yes?" Mistral shrugged. "I know you read fast, but you gotta stop hauling a pile of twenty or thirty books to your table. Those specialty magineering texts in particular! If there's a volume missing in the middle, I pretty much always find it in your pile."

"Oh…s-sorry, I'll try and reshelve more often."

"Thanks. Books are a shared asset."

Fresh off that sensible advice, Mistral turned his attention elsewhere. He hadn't been trying to start stuff but was merely saying hi to some familiar faces. This caught Oliver off guard until another student approached.

"I anticipated your presence here."

A female student, eyes hidden behind her bangs, flanked by two companions. Unlike Mistral, she was unmistakable.

"Ms. Ames…," Oliver said, turning to face her.

"A pleasure, Mr. Horn."

A well-mannered greeting. He considered this for a moment and elected to voice a complaint.

"…The match wound up being a fine experience, but three-on-one was certainly nerve-racking. Whether team or individual, I hope we next fight one-on-one."

"If you desire it, gladly. I no longer have anything to hide from you."

There was a hint of self-deprecation in her smile. Oliver was well aware she was referring to the power move she'd pulled at the end of their duel. While he debated how to respond, the girls on either side of Ames pounced.

"Hey, hey, hey—don't get cocky, Mr. Horn. We all know that win was a fluke."

"Damn straight! Next time, our Jaz is gonna take you down."

The rest of Team Ames clearly held a grudge. Oliver was left even more at a loss, but Nanao folded her arms, looking serious.

"Mm, indeed. Had her companions been as formidable as Ames herself, our victory would have been in doubt."

""Gah!""

The Azian girl meant no insult by this, but it eviscerated both lackeys like a *naginata* strike. They staggered backward. Ames sighed and stepped out from their shadow.

"Calm yourselves, ladies. I apologize on my companions' behalf. I'm afraid I have been too soft on them in the past."

"Aughhhh…"

"Sorry, Jaz! Sorry we're so weak!"

Tears in their eyes, each companion clung to one of Ames's sleeves. Oliver was starting to find their antics…heartwarming. They'd clearly been together awhile. These two were a bit deferential, which likely reflected their families' relationships with Ames's.

Ames patted both their heads, then faced forward again.

"Oh, and…Mr. Horn, Mr. Leik—and if possible, Mr. Reston. What would you say to sharing a private meal with me in the near future?"

"? I wouldn't mind, but…you mean to go over the match?"

Oliver wasn't sure what to make of this invitation. But beneath her bangs, a smile played on Ames's lips.

"That excuse suits me well. My family is old but of little fame. It is high time I started laying the groundwork for marriage."

The last word made the air freeze instantly. Oliver quickly stepped between her and Pete.

"Y-you may do as you like with Leik, but not Pete."

"…I mean, I wasn't going to accept, but why are *you* turning her down for me?"

"It's too soon for you!"

"Again, who asked *you*?"

Pete's protests hit him in the back, but Oliver refused to budge. A puff of air escaped Ames's nostrils.

"Apologies. Perhaps that was too aggressive. I shall reissue the invite at a later occasion."

Backing off, she turned to go. Her companions followed, hissing, "We never forget!" "Watch yourself on a moonless night!" Oliver and his group were left feeling rather bowled over.

"...That escalated quickly," Guy said. "But I guess it's about that time, huh? Next year, we'll all be in the upper forms."

"...Hmph..."

He seemed to take things in stride, but there was a small grumble from the curly-haired girl next to him. He glanced down and found her cheeks puffed up.

"? What're you sulking about, Katie? No one's going anywhere."

"...She didn't mention your name, Guy."

"Huh? Ah, right, she didn't. Guess I didn't meet her standards, sadly."

"Oh, so you *did* want her after you!"

"I didn't say that! What are you *actually* mad about?"

Katie's intense badgering left Guy backing away, and Chela was forced to intervene.

"Hold that bickering for now—they're about to start."

They followed her gaze and saw an upperclassman at the podium. Everyone quickly took their seats. Eyes like daggers, the dark-skinned Watch veteran scanned the faces of the assembled third-years and began speaking.

"Lesedi Ingwe, seventh-year. Godfrey's recuperating, so until he's up and about, I'm proxy president. I imagine many of you are confused by the unexpected invite, but let me first thank you for coming."

Her gratitude didn't ease their tension at all.

"If it helps settle your nerves, the Watch won't be forcing you to do anything. This is simply a request for aid. But to be clear, it's an extremely urgent one. The matter affects every student at Kimberly. And since you're all backing Godfrey, this isn't someone else's problem."

Whatever this was about, it seemed they had a right to refuse. That itself was a comfort, and they settled in to hear her out.

"Let me start from the top. You all know how Godfrey sustained his injury. The wound itself will heal over time, but the recovery will take a long while. That's less than good. His term may be almost over, but he's still got work to do."

She didn't need to explain what that work entailed. Everyone here knew. One look at Kimberly's history told you the combat-league victor's speech had huge pull with voters, and with the race as close as this one, that alone could decide the outcome. If he wanted the next president to be his successor, Godfrey *had* to win the league. And his supporters needed that to happen.

"There's only one way to heal his wound faster: steal the bone back from Cyrus Rivermoore. Which takes me to why we've called you here."

The name she dropped made everyone tense up again. A student in one corner called out, "You want us to help recover the bone?"

"Exactly. I'm sure you've worked it out by now, but there were two factors that got you an invite here. First, you're all Godfrey supporters. And second, you've all made it to the main round of the combat league. In other words, you're officially the best fighters in the third year. Bluntly speaking, we think you're capable of holding your own in a labyrinth fight."

Oliver had figured as much. Andrews's team was absent because they didn't meet the first requirement, and the second-year teams had simply been deemed not strong enough.

As it started adding up, Ames raised her hand.

"…That is an honor, but may I ask why you've gone with underclassmen against a force of Rivermoore's level? This seems like a concern that would normally be handled by the Watch alone, or at least be kept to the upper forms."

"You're hitting us where it hurts, but the answer's pretty simple. We're trying to avoid the upperclassmen directly clashing over Godfrey's bone. Not mincing words here—if that happens, people will die. We're gonna have the bulk of the older students stay on campus, indicating they ain't part of the search—which also warns the other side's upperclassmen off labyrinth delving themselves. This idea is to avoid an all-out war neither side desires. And they've shaken on that deal." She went on. "Plus, with the election in full swing, we've gotta be on guard against unexpected 'accidents' before the match date. That's an additional duty on top of what the Watch usually handles—which means we've got limited staff to put on the bone search."

By *"accidents,"* she clearly meant sabotage by the old student council. A shiver ran down Oliver's spine when he imagined the titanic struggle raging just out of sight even as they spoke. He couldn't help but remember that mess in the broom league last year.

"So we're committing minimal older students to the search. Given the scope of the area we need to cover, they alone may not get anywhere. That's where you come in. With me so far?"

Lesedi broke off, scanning the room. When no one asked a question, she got down to brass tacks.

"Obviously, not enough information to commit. So let me expand."

"First, while I said you're capable of holding your own, that doesn't mean we expect you to go up against Rivermoore himself. That would be insane. What we want from you is help covering more ground and the pressure on Rivermoore that causes. You've been through the team battles, so I'm sure you catch my drift."

If you wanted to corner your prey, numbers were a big advantage. Oliver's team had learned that the hard way when all three teams came after them, but everyone here was well aware. The third-years stood no chance going up against Cyrus Rivermoore themselves, but that meant they could stick to surveillance and support and do a lot to improve the search's efficacy.

"And we won't be sending you down there on your own. We'll be running four-man cells, and each of those will have an upperclassman to supervise. Who that is may change day by day, but assume you'll mostly be operating with your combat-league team plus one of us. That keeps the risk to a minimum, and if shit does go south, the upperclassman'll bear the brunt while you guys get outta there."

So each three-person team was effectively going to be treated as one real asset. Oliver felt that showed some real discretion on the Watch's part. No matter how up against the wall they were here, they weren't about to stick the younger students in harm's way. A core belief under-pinning Lesedi's whole speech.

"We'll start tomorrow night and go as long as three weeks. We have, of course, narrowed down the search perimeter—namely, where in the labyrinth Rivermoore is hiding. But to prevent outside interfer-ence, we're not disclosing that information until you've indicated your participation. Assume threat levels equivalent to the third and fourth layers and more undead than magical beasts. That's about all I'll say here. If you're scared of spooky stuff, best to drop out now."

Lesedi flashed them a grin. But she was only half joking—this was also a test. She was seeing if the kids here were ready to go up against the undead. That required less fighting technique than it did mental stability—if your mind was made of Swiss cheese, they'd get their fin-gers stuck in it. Get possessed or driven mad, and you could well prove a greater threat than the undead themselves.

The third-years were forced to weigh the threat levels against their own strengths.

Scowling, Mistral muttered, "Given what we're up against…I'd love to say the reward ain't worth the risk. But the times being what they are…we're the ones in trouble if the president stays down."

"We should help, not quibble," Stacy chimed in. "Unless we want Kimberly to be even worse next year."

She was a Cornwallis, an old family of some repute—but also a child of the main family branch, the McFarlanes. That left her following Chela's lead here and supporting Godfrey.

"I appreciate that sentiment," Lesedi said, smiling. "But don't worry about the reward. You aren't Watch members, and we'd have a lot of nerve asking you to risk your lives without any payment. Besides, this is Kimberly. The idea of asking mages to help based on goodwill and sound morals ain't just futile, it's legit disturbing."

She made a show of shuddering, then leaned forward.

"Five hundred thousand advance each, another on success. Godfrey's team wins the league, we'll put another five hundred thousand belc on top of that. Still ain't squat compared to the league prizes, but it's a heck of a lot better than your allowance. Plus—while the operation's in effect, you'll get firsthand instruction from your upperclassman supervisor. To some of you, that might be worth more than gold."

A murmur went through the room. Even if the search failed to pay off and they were left with only the advance, that was pretty good pay for three weeks' work.

"...No take backs?" a member of Team Mistral asked.

"None."

Lesedi followed that with a spell. A number of purses flew from the sack at her seat, scattering around the room and dropping before each student with the distinctive sound of metal against metal. They opened them up and found heaps of coins inside.

"If you're in, keep it. If you're not, leave it. If you need time, swing by the Campus Watch Headquarters when you've made up your minds. I swear by Godfrey's and the Watch's names, there will be no penalties for refusing. That is, if the Watch even exists next year."

Lesedi put her wand back on her hip. The purses in everyone's hands carried far more weight than the coins within.

"One last thing to help you decide. We've got a lot of experience with these situations, and it's our belief that Cyrus Rivermoore has *not* been consumed by the spell. There's not even any indication he might be on the brink of it. He is now and will be in full possession of his faculties. Up to you what you make of that. A mad beast and a rational one each pose a threat, and the discrepancy is not easily measured. And our goal is to back that beast into a corner."

She clearly had no intention of hiding the dangers here. Oliver thought that was indicative of the Watch's sincerity, but they were also honest to a fault. Candor could often work against you in the hellscape of Kimberly. And their opposition—Percival Whalley—had frequently slammed them for it.

"......"

But to his mind, this was *why* he believed their ambitions worth preserving. For that reason, he took the purse and stuffed it in his pocket. His eyes met Lesedi's, and she grinned.

"One question!" Yuri said, pocketing his own purse.

Lesedi turned toward him. "Yes, Mr. Leik?"

"I've been looking into this, and I believe that over the years, Rivermoore has gathered enough bones to form a *complete human body*. With that in mind—do you have any theories as to what drives him? Or what his purpose is?"

That certainly sent a stir around the room. Even Lesedi frowned.

"First I've heard of it. What's the basis of your assumption?"

"I went through the Watch records on students Rivermoore's attacked and, wherever possible, spoke to the student involved. I made a list of the bones they lost and found not a single duplicate. Here's the specifics."

Yuri pulled a wad of paper out of his pocket and, with a wave of his wand, sent it to the podium. Lesedi caught it, and as her eyes scanned the list, her expression turned grim.

"...Slipped right under our noses, huh?" she muttered. "Stealing bones was just what he did, and we never even thought to question it. Much less notice something this obviously systematic."

She tapped her knuckles against her temple. Once she'd finished reading, she looked up at Yuri.

"We'll go over this data in detail and task reliable necromancers with analyzing it. I'll have to answer your question later, Mr. Leik, but I appreciate your bringing this to our attention. I'm genuinely impressed you managed to get this many to talk."

"I was very persistent. Eight of them tried to kill me."

"You're thick-skinned!" She flashed him a smile. "Join the Watch once this is all over. We'll work you to the bone."

With that, she turned to the rest of the room.

"Unexpected intel aside, that's all we've got to say here. The operation details will be shared later on, exclusively with those who decide to join in. For that reason, I'm requesting your answers no later than noon tomorrow. Even if you accepted the reward on the spot, should you change your mind before then, feel free to return it. No one will mock or accost you for it. Be sure you're making the right decision."

Outside the classroom, the Sword Roses headed to the Fellowship for dinner. They found Miligan there, campaigning. Her stump speech over, she joined their table, and when they mentioned the search for Rivermoore, she bounded to her feet.

"Aha! That calls for *me*!" she cried.

Another girl swiftly put her in a full nelson—Lynette Cornwallis. The relationship they'd formed dealing with Salvadori had proved lasting, and she was now instrumental to Miligan's campaign.

"Are you nuts? You're running for president! You've already got a target on your back! I'm not letting you delve into the labyrinth *at all*, much less waste your time dealing with anything not directly campaign-related! Or do you *want* to find yourself face-to-face with Echevalria himself?!"

"Please! I want to teach these children! Hone their skills, make them strong, stomp the competition in the finals! Then feast my eyes on the look on Mr. Whalley's face!"

"Y-you don't even *try* to disguise it! You get just one taste of teaching and… Stace! Help! I've gotta drag this dumbass outta here!"

"Very well. Chela, I'll be right back."

"I'll help."

Stacy and Fay pitched in, and the Snake-Eyed Witch was dragged out of the room, kicking and screaming.

Watching them go, Guy muttered, "…Yeah, that was never happening. Can't have her along."

"Unfortunately, no." Oliver agreed. "The whole operation is about ensuring a Watch candidate wins, so we can't very well expose that candidate to any real danger."

Pete leaned in. "Forget the upperclassmen—what about us? Are we in?"

Everyone exchanged glances. Oliver had already made up his mind, so he spoke first.

"...I've accepted the reward already, so I certainly intend to. Even without the election factor, I owe Godfrey a few favors. It's a good chance to pay those back."

"I just wanna meet Rivermoore, so obviously I'm in," Yuri added.

"An earnest request from our honored predecessors. No true warrior would refuse, nor shall I."

Nanao showed no hesitation, so Pete turned his gaze to Chela, who nodded.

"Stace is in, so I am, too. I'm sure Mr. Willock will join us."

"So both your teams are all in," Guy said, focusing. "Guess we'll have to make up our minds, then."

Pete turned to him, and Katie folded her arms, thinking.

"I do want President Godfrey recovering soon...but are we actually up to the task? We're not gonna be in the way or anything? I mean, we made it to the main round, but we're hardly on the same level as Oliver and Nanao..."

"We don't need to be," Pete said. "Ms. Ingwe said they don't need us to fight; they need us to widen the ground they cover. If we weren't good enough, they'd never have brought us in. Personally, I'd like to go. That half a million belc alone is highly tempting, and I'm curious what we can learn from them."

Everything he said made sense to Katie, but she didn't seem quite ready to commit.

Guy put his hands on her shoulders. "All right, then, we're in," he said.

Surprised, Katie turned to look at him.

"Wh-what? We're just settling it that easily? Pete and I are always hard up, but you're fine on cash! No need to make us drag you into— Eek!"

Rather than let her finish, he'd stuck his hand into her hair and was busy messing it up. As she struggled, he made a face.

"Why would I *not* want money? Always nice to have. And that settles it!"

"What's that got to do with my hair?!"

"You had it coming."

With that, he finally let go of her head, and she huffily started straightening it back out.

Watching this with a smile, Oliver put a hand to his chin.

"My concern is how the old council will act. I can't imagine they'll sit idly by, but they're likely just as shorthanded. If our side is calling in the third-years, then right about now..."

"Thus, the plan is to locate Rivermoore and steal Godfrey's bone before the Watch can. Any questions?"

In a classroom on the third floor—not the one the Watch had used—Leoncio Echevalria was running a meeting with much the same goal. The students before him were also primarily third-years who had qualified for the main league: all teams Lesedi had left off her list because she knew they were backing his camp. Among them were Team Liebert, who'd traded blows with Team Horn, and Team Andrews, who'd steamrolled over Team Aalto.

Once Leoncio had completed his rundown of the request, a third-year at the back hesitantly raised his hand.

"One question...is participation mandatory?"

"We're only asking for voluntary cooperation. Though I hardly think refusing would be wise."

"Then I am out," Rossi said. He had his legs up on a front-row desk, his tone as dismissive as his posture. "This election 'as no relevancy to my life. 'andle your own mess in the background; I do not care."

Everyone else fidgeted uncomfortably, but Leoncio just grinned.

"Suit yourself. But what about your teammates?"

He glanced to the boys on either side of Rossi. The larger one—Joseph Albright—spoke up, his voice tinged with resignation.

"...I'm in. Can't ignore a request from an Echevalria."

"Spoken like a true Albright." Leoncio smirked. "You know your place better than that stray dog."

He'd known full well Albright had no choice in the matter. They both came from old conservative clans, and their families were closely linked, working together in any number of fields. Joseph Albright was in no position to do anything that could jeopardize that relationship.

Leoncio stepped down from the podium, advancing slowly on the audience. He stopped beside the third row.

"What about you, Mr. Andrews? Yours is an old family—will you happily lend a hand or waste your time howling?"

There was a brief silence.

"...I'll help," Andrews said at last. "But only until the main round of the senior leagues is done. From that point on, success or not, I'll pull out to focus on our final match. My teammates with me."

He demonstrated cooperative intent while also drawing a clear line. Leoncio's grin broadened; he clearly approved.

"Settled on baring your fangs, mm? That shows promise."

With that, he lost interest, returning his gaze to Rossi. Even the back of the Ytallian's head looked annoyed.

"Two have shown their mettle. I ask you once more, Mr. Rossi. Will you tuck your tail between your legs and cower off alone?"

The click of a tongue echoed. With his team on board, Rossi's objections meant little. Joining in and helping the search end early would likely be more productive. He knew that, and he could not let the taunt stand, so he spat, "Fine! 'ave it your way. On one condition: Whatever supervisor you stick us with—let it not be *you*."

"That is a shame," Leoncio muttered, moving back to the podium. "I'd have loved to tame you."

A shiver ran down Rossi's spine, and he quietly stood up before moving to a seat in the back row.

*   *   *

His recruitment complete, Leoncio left the classroom. In the hall, a figure slipped up behind him. A pale hand upon his shoulder, whispers in his ear.

"An unexpected windfall, giving you an advantage. I imagine the chortles never cease."

An elf's angular features and a sinister smile.

Yet, Leoncio's palm slammed into the wall, cracks spreading like a spiderweb.

"…Like picking up a trophy that's fallen from the shelf. What could be more tedious?"

"Haaa-ha. Let's dig a little deeper, shall we? Why are you so cross? If Rivermoore had come for you, we'd be the ones in trouble—is that what you're thinking?"

"No," Leoncio snapped. "Even caught off guard in those circumstances, I would not have allowed him to snatch my bone. Ordinarily, Godfrey would not have, either."

Khiirgi considered this a moment, then clapped her hands together.

"Oh! I see… I get it! This is what you're thinking—Godfrey failed to escape the ambush because his mind was on protecting *everyone* there. You included."

No sooner had this left her mouth than Leoncio's hand disappeared. Athame drawn too fast for the eye to see, it was piercing her robe, pressed against her shoulder.

"Watch your mouth, Alp. I'm not in the best mood, and you may find yourself down an arm because of it."

"Go ahead," she purred, intoxicated. "What's an arm or two when I can see that look on your face?"

Realizing his emotions were only giving her pleasure, Leoncio's expression vanished, and his blade returned to its scabbard. Khiirgi let out a disconsolate moan, then put her hand on his shoulder again.

"It may not sit right with you, but the fact that you won't let that take precedence over electoral victory is laudable. Prevent Godfrey's restoration, win the league, and that will secure Percy's victory. You're good with that?"

"It need not be said." His voice was calm again. "I'm placing you in charge of our labyrinth efforts. For now, feel free to forget the league altogether. If Godfrey's not in play, Gino and I can handle the other two."

His rivalry with Godfrey might have been a fixation, but if he could use this to influence the election, he would not hesitate. These background schemes were Leoncio Echevalria's bread and butter. If he could win before the match began, that simply meant Godfrey had not been a worthy opponent. Tamping down the emotions born from that idea, he focused on the issue at hand.

"If it's as easy as getting the bone first, splendid. If Rivermoore's resistance makes that impossible, then run interference on the Watch—do your best to keep it indirect. If we're too blatant about it, that could lose us votes and reflect poorly on Percy's character."

"I'm well aware. We're simply recovering Godfrey's stolen bone on his behalf. And it just so happens that'll result in it getting back to him a tad later."

Khiirgi's rationale was so transparent, it made him snort. As of yet, Godfrey's backers hadn't wavered. The way he'd fought against Vanessa Aldiss was every bit as imposing as his title; for now, the students were more inclined to criticize Rivermoore for the cowardly backstabbing. But if Leoncio's side recovered the bone first, that might change. That would suggest the Watch without Godfrey lacked real leadership—and would prove the strength of the new council a vote for Percival Whalley would ensure.

"The election's drawing to a close. I won't forbid you your enthusiasms, but don't lose track of our priorities. Bring Percy back some good news, Khiirgi. No matter how out of character that is."

There was an unprecedented weight behind this order. Khiirgi's lips curled like a scimitar—and her figure vanished like mist.

CHAPTER 2

Kingdom of the Dead

Seven PM, a darkened classroom on the Kimberly main building's first floor. Several figures stood before a large mirror on the wall.

"Everyone here? First, thanks for making this choice."

Before the mirror stood a seventh-year girl, Lesedi Ingwe. Around her were Tim and the other Watch members and every third-year from the meeting the day before. The Sword Roses were among them, albeit in separate groups.

"There's a lot of us, so we're gonna split into squads and head to our destination that way. With these numbers, dividing your forces is standard procedure for labyrinth traversal. Crowds just provoke the labyrinth ecosystem and bring unexpected trouble. Worth remembering. Move out!"

With that abrupt conclusion, Lesedi nodded to the other squad leaders. Half took their teams through the mirror, and the other half headed out through a different entrance. Katie's and Chela's teams were with the latter group. Oliver caught their eyes one last time—a promise they'd come back safe. Then Lesedi approached him.

"Team Horn, I'll be your supervisor today. I saw how you all moved in the match, and I'm expecting good things."

"We'll do what we can," said Oliver. "But Ms. Ingwe, shouldn't you be prepping for the main match?"

"If our first match was against Echevalria, I wouldn't be here. But it ain't. Still a little luck on our side."

She grinned and turned back to the mirror. Oliver, Nanao, and Yuri followed her through. After a few seconds of darkness, they were thrown out into the dim halls of the labyrinth.

"Shaaa!"

A warg had launched itself at them, but Lesedi's roundhouse kick tore into it. The head exploded, sending brain matter everywhere. Remembering the senior-league prelim, Oliver shuddered for more than the obvious reason—Vanessa Aldiss had shrugged *this* off?

"Careful," Lesedi warned. "All those alterations they did for the prelim have the beasts in a bad mood."

"A most impressive kick!" Nanao said, delighted.

Lesedi ran off, never even glancing at the warg's corpse. They followed. Passing through the first layer, Oliver voiced a question.

"...Same style? As President Godfrey, I mean?"

"Well spotted. Keen eye."

She grinned at him. Seeing them still keeping up just fine, she upped the pace a bit, expanding on her answer.

"I'm the one who taught him a few tricks. These martial arts have been passed down in my family for generations, rooted in a style the ordinaries developed. Naturally, we've brought in sword arts techniques, blending the two and making it more effective."

That made sense. Her skin was significantly darker than Chela's, suggesting her roots were not of this continent. Those distinctive leg-based moves likely hailed from there, too.

"You're orthodox Lanoff style, so it might just seem heretical. But it's got real advantages against mages. Must have put some ideas in his head—your Rossi was after me to teach him. I did what he asked, gave him five or six good kicks, and he went home satisfied."

"...That does sound like him." Oliver sighed.

He'd been very aware that Rossi was devouring Koutz at a prodigious speed, but it sounded like he was adding to his bag of dirty tricks as well. The overhead kick he'd used against Pete on the water in the lake district likely hailed from there. That would make him even tougher to handle in the future.

They kept talking, avoiding the magic traps in the halls without anyone needing them pointed out. Lesedi was keeping a close eye on their movements, figuring out their predilections and how they fitted her own tendencies.

"Not a good match for Hibiya's flow. These moves would best suit you, Leik."

"Oh? Like this?"

Mid-strike, Leik smoothly sent his body spinning into a kick—an improved copy of the kick Lesedi had used against the warg. A fundamentally different physical demand than anything found in the three main schools, but his reproduction was uncannily good. Lesedi's eyes narrowed.

"Yeah...but you sure pick things up creepily fast. What's your base?"

"Don't have one! If pressed, I guess stuff I gleaned racing around the mountains."

"Huh...? Not sure I follow, but you mean...less trained skills than a freakish knack? Fine, that makes it all the more worth honing."

Lesedi flashed her teeth. Yuri had clearly met with her approval—which was a relief to Oliver. For all his good cheer, Yuri's personality was not for everyone. Like Rossi, some people instantly despised him—so Lesedi not being one of them was cause for rejoicing. Odds were they'd end up in mortal peril together eventually.

"No matter what the labyrinth throws at us, the three of you can likely handle it through the third layer. But it'll be a different story on the fourth. Strength alone ain't enough."

"...We're going deeper? Where is this place?"

Oliver sounded dubious. Any deeper than the Library of the Depths and the threat level skyrocketed—worse, they'd hit the trial at the Library Plaza. He'd made it through there once with Karlie and Robert, but this party couldn't handle it like that. They'd need an alternate strategy.

Catching the demand in his look, Lesedi snorted.

"Hard question to answer, there. Lemme start with this pretext—the labyrinth is not necessarily always a one-way path *down*. There's the vertical progression from first layer to second, second to third, but a number of strata also have *side branches*."

"Hmm? Constructed like an ant's colony, you mean?" Nanao asked.

"Close enough, yeah. But we're talking about a stupid-huge labyrinth here. Even Kimberly ain't got the resources to manage all these branches. Places deemed lacking in benefits or not worth the cost get sealed and left to rot. They're what we call the labyrinth's abandoned zones."

Their pace never once slowed. The stone-paved paths gave way to the bustling forest. From that point on, all fell silent. For a while, they stayed cautious. They were used to what this place typically offered, but there was no guarantee there weren't deep monsters brought up for the prelims still lingering around. Still on their guard, they slipped through the forest's gloom.

"...Calmer than I expected," Oliver said, taking it in.

The faculty had clearly put in the work to restore things. The second-layer beasts were having a few territorial conflicts, but otherwise there were no obvious changes. They'd likely evacuated the original residents somewhere before bringing in the more powerful beasts. Oliver couldn't begin to imagine how, but possibly all it would take was a howl from Vanessa Aldiss.

Once over the irminsul, they were almost to the end of the layer. The trees thinned, and there was no more risk of ambush. That loosened Lesedi's lips.

"Back to the abandoned zones. Ordinarily, students never venture into them. Nothing to be gained by going there. But there are exceptions. Like if you come in equipped with extraordinary magical techniques that let you remodel those vast spaces to your liking, making a garden all your own."

All present had cleared the Battle of Hell's Armies, so they blew right past it, into the marshes of the third layer. Lesedi was clearly taking them on a different path than the one leading to the fourth stratum, and they assumed this led to the branch in question. Her back to them, Lesedi continued her lecture.

"Rivermoore did just that. You can't even call that thing a workshop. By the time we noticed, it was already his kingdom. One where he's the only living thing. A kingdom populated entirely by the undead."

Imagining what that meant, Oliver gulped. He was picturing the third layer under Ophelia Salvadori's control: the native beasts gone, replaced by grotesque chimeras, the very air filled with her maddening perfume. Rivermoore's territory was on that scale, yet he had put far more time and effort into creating it. How horrifying it must be.

They pushed through the tall grass around the swamp and saw a dark cave yawning up ahead. Lesedi plunged straight in, and the others followed. Yet—

"Mm?"

"Oh, a dead end?"

—five minutes into the cave, having taken several forks, they hit a wall. Wrong turn, perhaps? Before they could ask, Lesedi waved her athame at the rock face...

"Fragor!"

...and blew the wall down. This was hardly anything as fancy as a secret entrance; she'd simply used brute force to open a hole to the other side. Dust flew, and air rushed out—singularly stale air. The feel of it on their skin made one fact clear: They were entering the warlock's domain.

Athames swiftly in hand, the group advanced beyond the blast site. Bathed in a glow, white like moonlight, was a vast gray land on which sprouted countless bones in lieu of grass. The hole behind them sealed on its own, and the flow of air died—no winds at all. A spectacle that went beyond sinister into the downright unreal, like they'd stepped from their world into the next.

"Brace yourselves," Lesedi growled. "Border patrol incoming."

All three made ready for battle. The bones scattered across the ground were quivering...and soon sprang to life, putting themselves together, assembling into a towering form. Blocking their path was a thirty-foot-tall three-headed beast—the bones of a cerberus.

"These ain't like magic beasts or chimeras. You know where to aim?" Lesedi asked. She stood at the fore, unperturbed, her arms folded.

Making swift observations of their foe's appearance, Oliver said, "Can't expect blood loss or organ damage, so if there's a weakness, it must be the bones driving its mobility. With this creature, severing the spine seems effective."

"Correct. A good start. I'll get in close and draw its attention. Take your time lining up the shot if you need it, but hit that back hard."

Short and sweet. She was already charging in. Oliver, Nanao, and Yuri spread out, moving into position. The lifeless cerberus released a howl, as if dictating the laws of this realm, as if rebuking the arrogance of the living.

At the same time, the other squads were smashing into the abandoned zone.

"Frigus!"

"Flamma!"

Pete's and Guy's spells flew at the bone beast's spine. Ice and fire spells at once, exploiting the temperature gap to weaken the target. Mentally giving their performance a passing grade, their supervisor— Tim "Toxic Gasser" Linton—was busily opening and closing the lid on his hip pouch.

"Tch...babysitting is *so* not my thing! How am I supposed to use any decent poison?"

While his struggle may have been internal, his muttering reached their ears and made the younger students all the more intent on taking this creature out before poison was needed. But that was easier said than done. Each step Guy took, his soles told him this land was dry as a bone, not a drop of moisture anywhere.

"Soil this parched, tool plants aren't happening—how you doing, Katie?"

Certain one of his strengths wasn't an option here, Guy shot a question over his shoulder. Since the battle began, Katie had been drawing an elaborate diagram on the ground.

"…I'm good," she answered with a nod. "It links up."

She sounded confident. She went down on her knees by the magic circle and began chanting.

"Come to me, Marco, Lyla. **Sequitor.**"

The circle activated, lighting up—and a wind began to blow. A gust across a windless plain—proof she'd opened a gate to elsewhere. Katie's diagram was a bridge between two separate points in space, and across that bridge came two figures: Marco, a troll in heavy armor wielding a hammer, and Lyla, a griffin with a saddle on her back.

"Damn, nice pawns you got there. How come you didn't use these in the league?" Tim snorted.

Forcing back the exhaustion of the massive mana expenditure, Katie managed, "They're not much good for stealth. Didn't want to trot them out just to use as a distraction."

The ground shook as the troll and griffin advanced on either side of her. The pact she'd formed with her familiars established a channel to them; by temporarily expanding that, she was able to summon them to her location. It took a lot out of her, but the advantages of having large familiars around more than made up for that.

"And one more thing—they aren't pawns. They're my friends."

A skelebeast, sharp claws flailing, two figures dashing around beneath its feet. One was the upper-forms supervisor and the other a third-year,

Rosé Mistral. While the monster chased them around, the other three were casting spells from outside claw range. The beast staggered, and the *real* Mistral grinned.

"Hya-ha! Adorable! So easily fooled!"

"Impetus! Back in the habit, huh?"

"Can't be acting all sedated when we're up against something this spooktacular! I had nightmares 'bout the display skeletons in my mom's workshop as a kid! Ahhh, the horror, the horror, would that I had a blanket to hide beneath!"

Despite his claims, his control over his splinter never once wavered. The older student backing that play was suitably impressed. The illusion of extra numbers made it far easier for her to be out front—especially since, unlike flesh-and-blood juniors, there was *no* need to protect a splinter.

A massive tail swung into a sweeper blow. A third-year girl ducked smoothly under that, delivering a counter slash at the base of the creature's tail, severing it. Down its greatest weapon, the beast flailed.

"It seems no tougher than the living ones," Jasmine Ames whispered. "Though I'm hardly an expert."

"You're our queen, Jaz!"

"We're kicking this thing's ass!"

Two burst spells hit the spine, snapping it, and the teammates flanking Ames struck a triumphant pose. But even as they celebrated, their supervisor pointed at the crumbling skeleton.

"Hate to burst your bubble, but it ain't done yet. Here's where it gets nasty."

They followed the upperclassman's finger…and found the bones reassembling. The broken spine now formed two columns, merging with the tail Ames had severed and producing two new skelebeasts. Ames's minions gaped.

"Huhhh?!"

"No fair! I call no fair!"

"...Fascinating," said Ames. "The bones rebuilding into new forms. That *is* 'nasty.'"

Four bony legs kicked the ground, pouncing on its quarry. A furious assault, but Rossi smoothly slipped past it. The approach itself was rather like what Teresa had demonstrated in the combat-league prelims, but his transparent lack of enthusiasm drew all the more ire.

"Ugh, do I 'ave to be 'ere? My 'eart is as empty as this skeleton's ribs."

"You speak as if you had depth to begin with. **Fragor!**"

Albright's spell hit the exposed flank, snapping off a chunk of the rib cage. Rossi kept baiting it as Andrews nodded.

"...You noticed it'll shape-shift, so you're damaging the bones first."

"It's clearly got a lot of extra bones the living ones don't have. Take it down wrong, we'll be stuck fighting *more*."

"Whatever! Fight 'ow you like."

All three nodded and kept going. The upperclassman watching them fight—Khiirgi Albschuch—had neither moved to help nor offered words of advice. She was simply watching their every move.

"Such skilled children. Haaa-ha. How tantalizing."

She licked her lips, and a shiver ran down all three spines. Their ally behind them was far more frightening than the foe in front—on that one point, the trio of third-years agreed.

Battles had broken out across the border, but since everyone spent time observing the unknown foes, nearly all squads wrapped up the fighting almost simultaneously.

Oliver's team had been up against the cerberus, and after one transformation and two takedowns, it was reduced to an unmoving heap of bones.

Arms folded, Lesedi nodded. "Solid first try. Good work."

Oliver was relieved to receive a passing grade.

Her gaze already past the fallen foe to the gray expanse beyond, Nanao sniffed the air.

"…No scent of life to be found," she said. "And yet, I sense maneuvers being made. An odd place indeed."

"You picked up on it? Yeah, this place is one of a kind. Hard to explain—best you feel it on your skin."

With that, Lesedi dropped her satchel to the ground. Then she opened it up, stuck her hand in, and pulled out four white lumps— each looked like some sort of skull, clearly far too large to actually fit in a satchel that size. No doubt they'd been magically folded into the space via a compression spell.

"First, put these on."

"Hrm? The skull of an ape?" Nanao asked.

"Taken from a demon ape's corpse, engraved with a sigil. To what purpose—?" Oliver asked, examining it.

Lesedi had already donned her skull, her eyes shining between the halves of its jaw.

"Like I said, this place is unique. In a graveyard, the living stand out among the throngs of the dead. Thus, if we act like we're dead, we'll have an easier time of it."

That all made sense. It was like wearing green and brown in the forest—a form of camouflage specific to this locale. It might look bizarre but was well worth it if fewer undead viewed them as hostiles.

Oliver put the skull on, and something poked him in the back. Wondering what that something was, he turned around—and found Nanao wearing her skull, arms held high yet limp at the wrists, her tongue hanging out.

"Oliver! Oliverrrr! How I abhor thee!"

"Wh-what? Did I do something wrong?"

"This is how specters are believed to act where I'm from. Abhorrrr!"

"Huh, that's neat! What were ghosts like back home again? Hmm…

Well, there was this one time I ran into a severed head dangling from a fruit tree."

This alarming anecdote came from Yuri, also bone-bedecked. With all her juniors fully equipped, Lesedi reshouldered her satchel and shrugged.

"These things won't work miracles. We cast any spells, that'll blow our cover quick, and this disguise won't work on any of the better familiars. But there's also a ton of sundry ghosts not directly under Rivermoore's control. They're likely the vast majority. If we can pass through while avoiding unnecessary fights, we'll conserve magic and energy."

This was hide-and-seek. Their focus clear, Lesedi led the way out into the wasteland. The younger students followed on her heels.

"If we're gonna find him, we need clues. First, let's locate a town."

"A town?!" Oliver yelped. That was the last word he'd expected.

Lesedi shot him a grin. "Don't be shocked. They may be dead, but they're *people*. And when people gather, they make towns."

Her words were neither metaphor nor exaggeration—as Katie's team had just discovered.

"...Wh-what in the...?"

There was a town smack in the middle of all that gray nothing. The entrance led directly to the main street, where throngs of dead roamed. There were shops and stalls set up on both sides, staffed by the dead, serving dead customers. In the center, carts pulled by bone horses threaded their way through the shuffling hordes.

Guy peered down the road, unable to stop his eye from twitching. "...Place is bustling, huh? I'd love to join in—if anyone here *wasn't* made of bones."

"They don't seem hostile...but what's this?" Pete asked. He squinted, observing a stall. "Are they buying and selling things? From one undead to another...?"

The wares in question seemed to be stones and bits of dried wood

of various shapes and sizes. The customers were paying for these…
with much the same things. Even without knowing what it was the
undead wanted, it seemed unlikely these transactions held any intrin-
sic meaning. And yet, they were going through the motions.

As his juniors gaped, Tim muttered, "Ever tried controlling the
undead? It's harder than you'd think. If you're simply pointing them at
someone, then you just rile up their lingering hatred. But if you need
them on standby, then you've gotta find a way to stabilize their emotions. Fail to do that, and the curse energy runs wild, or it wavers and
gets absorbed by those around it. With only a few of them, you can just
manage them directly, but with numbers this ridiculous, you've gotta
create a specialized environment or you'll never keep up. That's why
Rivermoore remodeled the whole abandoned zone as a place where
the undead can kick back and relax."

Pete folded his arms, pondering this. That would explain why there
was a town here. But that still left a more fundamental concern.

"…Wait," Katie said. "Then where'd they all come from? Even the
Scavenger couldn't bring this many undead in from outside. I wondered the same thing at the Battle of Hell's Armies…"

If there were no living, there were also no dead. These unnamed
undead before them and the spartoi fighting their never-ending battle—
both must once have been as alive as Katie was now. That was the primary difference between these creatures and magical beasts.

"So I'll come right out and ask," she said, casting Tim a sidelong
glance. "Who were these people?"

His eyes on the dead running errands ahead, he replied, "You
already know the answer. No one brought them in. So there's only one
place they could've come from—they were *always* here."

"…The Parsu," Oliver whispered, digging the word up from the far
corners of his memory. His team was on a plateau, staring down at a
different town from the one Katie and the others were visiting.

Lesedi caught his murmur, and a smile crossed her lips.

"I'm impressed. The Wild Geese's catcher's an archeologist, too, huh?"

"I just know a few scraps about history predating the founding of Kimberly. But I can't imagine another explanation. Since the labyrinth itself is a ruin of an ancient magic civilization, then it makes sense for the residents to be here."

Oliver was merely analyzing the sight before him. Meanwhile, Yuri had his arms folded and his head cocked.

"Hmm...? But do souls even stick around that long? I had it in my head they just, like, ascend after a while if you let 'em be."

"That's the general principle, yes. But that changes if they have particularly powerful convictions or if they're bound by a spell. This is likely the latter. They're not lingering; they're not *allowed* to leave. A magic contract forged in life keeps their souls here. Probably something only achievable via the magic of the time."

"...A pitiable plight," Nanao said, putting a name to the emotions swirling within.

Oliver felt tempted to agree, but he stifled the urge. Whatever lay in the past, what lay before them now was undoubtedly a land of death. It would not do to let empathy stay his blade. Telling himself as much, he spoke as if words would banish the turmoil within.

"...The years have taken their toll on these ghosts, and they have little mind remaining. From the look of the town, they're simply repeating routines from their lives, like children playing house. But the town itself is oddly modern. Even the style of the buildings isn't that old."

"Yeah, Rivermoore had the undead build all this," said Lesedi. "I heard this place was far worse before his arrival. Filled with the howls of the dead, their minds long since ground away, yet still incapable of ascending."

Even as the warlock robbed the living of their bones in the labyrinth, here he had spent a great deal of time making a place for the dead to dwell. Yet, imagining that brought still more questions—Oliver struck a thoughtful pose.

"…His purpose eludes me. All this work to re-create an ancient kingdom for the dead, but for what? Does it have anything to do with the students' bones?"

"That, I don't know, nor do I need to. No matter what he's after, we've got one job here: get Godfrey's bone back ASAP."

Lesedi had no time for doubts. And in her position, cutting those free made perfect sense. Oliver did not have that luxury. Yuri's reckless streak would not end until Rivermoore's purpose became clear.

As Oliver's brain churned, Lesedi took her eyes off the town, scanning their surroundings.

"You said the undead had no minds left, but that's not true for *all* of them. The exceptions are far trickier. If they're driven enough to survive a millennium—well, can you imagine how strong they are?"

That forced Oliver's mind back to the present. The skelebeasts they'd fought on entry had been but heralds, and there were far worse things out here—that was the gist of Lesedi's warning. Who knew how many?

"If we encounter one, we'll all need to do our part. If it proves too much, group up with a nearby squad or beat a temporary retreat. But we shouldn't run into all that many. The Watch and Rivermoore have clashed in the past, and we've taken out quite a few of the tougher ones. Even he can't replace those easily."

"Aha! You mean, this kingdom itself is pretty big, but he doesn't actually have enough strong units to cover it. That means he can't afford to use his valuable assets willy-nilly. He must have them carefully placed in important locations," Leik said, fearlessly getting right to the point.

Lesedi nodded. "Your team sure saves my breath. Yeah. Logically speaking, if we follow the trail of exceptional undead, we'll get closer to Rivermoore. Naturally, he'll have decoys out there, but the total number is finite, and he can't make more."

But that also meant they could not avoid fighting these undead. Oliver took a deep breath, steeling his nerve. Godfrey had been in predicaments like this on a daily basis. But he'd be graduating this year—and next year, Oliver himself would be in the upper forms. It was time to put his fears aside.

"Running around trying to find the strong undead is one plan, but there's a faster way to accomplish that goal," said Lesedi. "That's why we're here, looking down at the town. Anyone want to guess? I'll give you one hint—you had the same thing done to you recently."

Quickly solving that riddle, Oliver drew his white wand, the tip aimed squarely at the town below—and that was all it took for Nanao and Yuri to catch up. They matched his aim.

"...Not sure I can land an attack from this distance, so what say we use flashing lights and sound to draw them out?"

"Ha-ha! That'll work. No need to copy Ms. Ames. But remember this kinda thing crops up in real combat. Another lesson for ya."

Even as she lectured, Lesedi aimed her own wand. Her eyes were always laser-focused, but now they narrowed, gleaming like a bird of prey.

"The response won't take long. Be mindful of the direction and lag. **Magnus Fragor!**"

"""**Magnus Fragor!**"""

Katie's team, too, was hurling spells at some other town, trying to bait a powerful foe. Four burst spells sailed off, but rather than watch them land, Tim urged his team on.

"Okay, no lollygagging! Move! First law of sniping!"

"Urgh, I'm sorry, everyone...! Your lives looked so peaceful, too!"

"No time for guilt! We'll end up skeletonized, too!"

Guy's words hit Katie like a slap on the back. This wasn't a pleasant approach, but they were in Rivermoore's territory, and the undead in that town could turn on them at any time. Being wishy-washy would not help here. Katie nodded and kept running.

On their way to the next hiding spot, Pete called out, "Something's coming," his eyes off route.

Neither Katie nor Guy had sensed a thing, but in his female body, Pete's mana detection tended to get pretty accurate. And he was soon proven right—a few seconds later, Tim stopped in his tracks.

"That tingle on my skin—ha-ha! We got one, kids. A real winner."

No sooner had the words left his mouth than everyone could feel the mana density. All eyes turned to the horizon—and a plume of dust rose up, eventually revealing a herd of bone horses more than twenty strong. Each was ridden by a skeleton, but Tim's eyes were focused on the knight at the fore.

At least 50 percent larger than the others, it wore weathered plate armor like a general of yore, a massive halberd gripped in its hands. Beneath the helm, the sockets of its skull burned with fires that raged on, even in death. An obsession with battle, unbroken by the passage of time.

"Thank you, thank you. Showing up on the first day I'm around?" the Toxic Gasser teased. "...Always did regret not taking you down in my fourth year. Now I can pass the torch with a clear conscience!"

Tim gleefully reached for the pouch at his hip. Seeing the Toxic Gasser fired up, Katie, Guy, and Pete kept their distance—but they all drew their athames, prepared to face the oncoming threat.

Meanwhile, Oliver's team had followed similar tactics, moving from their spellcasting locale to a hiding spot in the sand. Not long after, *something* appeared in the skies above, surrounded by a flock of bone birds—clearly quite different from the skelebeasts they'd fought. A black-robed figure, its shoulders in the grasp of a large skelebird's talons. Two snakes grew from its body, and where the eyes and nose should be was a swirling black vortex, the sight of which made the hairs on the back of Oliver's neck stand on end.

"A zahhak…!"

"That's what they call 'em," Lesedi intoned. "Said to be the remnants of an ancient mage, but no one knows for sure. Given their tendency to roam ruins like these, they may originate in a tír migration. A creature of many mysteries, accurate categorization included."

Oliver had seen one himself, his first year, just before taking out Darius. He'd been aware he might run into one in the labyrinth someday but had never expected it to be a familiar. Further proof of how powerful Cyrus Rivermoore was.

"But we know how to beat 'em. This particular one's a first, but that just means I get to teach you the ABC's of killing 'em," Lesedi explained. "First, use a doublecant burst spell to bring down these birds. Match my cast on that."

All three nodded. Oliver began assessing the foes they were about to engage. Including the one carrying the zahhak, there were five large skelebirds. Around them flew roughly 120 midsize or small ones. These did not seem to pose a major threat, but there was a strong chance the birds would join together, reassembling into a more powerful foe. Taking out as many as they could with the first blast was a necessary measure to allow them to focus on the zahhak.

"Rule number one of fighting a powerful foe—before you strike, assume they have backup coming. Then set yourself a time limit. Here, let's go with five minutes. Even if the undead from town come running in, if we've pulled out by then, we'll get away clean."

As they waited for the flock to reach casting range, Lesedi continued her lecture. Aware of the enemy's detection range, she'd positioned them a fair distance from the town, giving them a comfortable margin before backup could come running in. If they failed to fell this foe within those five minutes, they'd turn tail and run. This plan prioritized survival over victory.

Conscious of that, Oliver's team dug into the sand, athames at the ready.

"Rule number two. Always strike first. **Magnus Fragor!**"

"""**Magnus Fragor!**"""

Four burst spells shot skyward. The zahhak spotted them, but it was too late to dodge. The explosion covered a wide area, taking most of the birds with it and shattering the wings of the large skelebird. It and the zahhak began to fall.

"Okay, activate the circle, then spread out and continue the aerial bombardment!"

Lesedi was already running toward the landing site. Oliver, Nanao, and Yuri aimed their athames in three separate directions, chanting—and activating the magic circle they'd inscribed ahead of time. This placed a dome-like barrier over Lesedi and the area; not that powerful, but combined with their suppressing fire, it would be enough to stave off the bone flock for now. The key here was to keep them from getting in Lesedi's way.

Shooting down the descending skelebirds, they kept one eye on her battle. After all, that was the real meat of Lesedi Ingwe's combat demonstration.

"**Impetus!** Shiiiiiaaahhhh!"

Lesedi's first strike was a gust spell. And although it did double duty as a feint, the spell wasn't aimed at the enemy. It created a current in the air she was running through, and she rode upon that, giving herself a boost of speed and a shift in direction her opponent couldn't anticipate. Her roundhouse kick hit the zahhak before it could recover from its landing. It tried to throw out a black barrier and block, but Lesedi's kick smashed through that and scored a direct hit on the zahhak's shoulder. It went flying, and she gave chase.

"Rule three! Don't let them recover! Once you've got the advantage, *keep it!*"

True to her word, before the zahhak could right itself, she was pummeling it with further kicks. At a glance, it might seem like a wild flurry, but she was smoothly weaving in a number of leg sweeps that kept it permanently off-balance. And each time it left itself exposed, her athame stabbed a weak point—and had just gouged a shallow groove out of its throat.

"Don't trade spells or slashes! Make that shit a one-sided beatdown! Prep three ways to finish it from your opening move!"

"…!"

Oliver gulped. This was a horrifically practical lesson. Completely ignoring the accepted practices of sword arts but rock-solid on the elements that decided a battle's outcome. A comprehensive grasp of fighting theory, readily broken away from as her own techniques and the situation at hand required.

"Such polish," Nanao muttered.

A curious choice of words, but Oliver got why she chose them. Lesedi had found her own style beyond what the book said and had refined it to perfection. It was painfully obvious why Rossi had sought her teachings.

"Shiii!" Lesedi roared.

The zahhak ducked under a flying spin kick to the head. But that big swing had been intentional and was followed by a backhanded slice, cutting off the zahhak's left arm at the root. This made Oliver grimace. Hiding the cut itself in the motion of the kick made this extremely hard to dodge. But holding a wand the wrong way around was, conventionally, a sign of surrender. A number of styles taught it as a dirty trick designed for a surprise kill, but Lesedi likely never even registered that aspect of it, only the functionality.

Perhaps a single arm counted as result enough—Lesedi broke off her one-sided rush. Switching her athame around to the proper grip, she took a step back, calling to her juniors behind.

"You see that? This is how you set the pace. The birds you dropped and the arm I severed—we're now starting at a clear advantage."

All three nodded. The results spoke for themselves. Her words came not from what she'd read in books but from what she'd learned by skirting certain death more times than she could count.

"Watching your league match, I got the strong impression all three of you tend to enjoy the fight a bit too much. But the nexus of a real fight is to never let your foe make a move. In that sense, I rate the other three teams higher."

"Mm, a tried-and-true principle of troop deployment," Nanao agreed.

Staring down the zahhak, Lesedi spared a quick glance at the sky. The spell barrage had been effective, and the bone birds were merely wheeling, showing no signs of descent. It seemed unlikely they feared getting shot down, so perhaps they'd simply learned they couldn't break the barrier and were waiting for an opening. They remained sinister, but at the very least, the group should be able to keep them away from the zahhak for the time being. In light of which, Lesedi moved to the next phase.

"Okay, let's trade places. I've weakened it a bit, so it should be solid practice for you. Take your time and get the hang of how it fights. If you're in trouble, I'll barge in—"

"Well, aren't you a proper teacher, Hard Knocker."

As the third-years stepped into the barrier and Lesedi out, an unexpected voice called to her. Oliver jumped, narrowing his eyes. The zahhak had no face, let alone a mouth. But that deep, masculine growl had come from the vortex swirling where the face should be.

"...Rivermoore," Lesedi replied, her brow furrowing. "Not how I expected to hear from you."

"Mwa-ha-ha-ha. It was just so heartwarming. You used to be as rabid as Bloody Karlie, but now you've actually learned how to *mentor*."

"You just here to ooze spite? Then I don't care. Cut the connection."

Lesedi waved a hand dismissively. The warlock in the vortex chuckled.

"No, that's just a side benefit. I'm about to disrupt your lesson and felt I should drop a warning. **Deformatio.**"

On the spell's cue, the zahhak's body began to creak, transforming. The bones within rearranged themselves—even sprouting a new arm.

Lesedi gritted her teeth. "What the hell? You've even meddled with a zahhak?!"

"Doing my part to represent the upper forms. Can't show off to my juniors just using what was lying around."

The transformation complete, the zahhak's physical and magical abilities now projected an entirely different threat. The warlock's speech continued.

"This, too, is a product of ancient necromancy. Or you could call it a failed attempt at a life-prolongment spell—if you're curious, read my upcoming dissertation on the subject. If you can make it back to campus alive."

With that, Rivermoore's voice cut out. Lesedi had her eyes locked on the zahhak, ready for anything.

"…Change of plans. The three of you are on backup. Unknown enemies pose a serious threat. Always exercise the utmost caution."

"Verily."

"Shame. This looks fun!"

Nanao and Yuri both nodded, faced with the new zahhak. Blue light started pouring from its back—a sphere, armful size, floating above it.

"…A floating ball of light…"

It was a bit like the false moon Cornwallis had used their first year. Oliver observed this carefully, but it seemed to offer no attack options on its own. Before his watchful eyes, the glowing orb moved soundlessly to a position behind the zahhak…

"Below us!"

The light had extended the zahhak's shadow toward their feet. The group leaped back when Lesedi barked a warning—and the next moment, spear-like blades shot out of the shadow itself.

The threat identified, Lesedi yelled, "Shadow Crawl! Watch out for attacks from its shadow!"

"Will shining some light help? **Lumina!**"

Yuri acted on instinct. White light bathed the ground and canceled out the oncoming shadow.

"Simple but effective. Surround it in all directions—"

But before Lesedi could finish, the sphere behind the zahhak split, rising upward and rejoining up above—projecting shadows from the bone birds wheeling below it.

"Not that easy, huh? Well-planned, Rivermoore."

Shadows were flitting in every direction, and Lesedi clicked her tongue. But she'd already made her choice. Pushing back the shadows with the light of her spell, she yelled, "Rule four! If the risk outweighs your odds of winning, bail! If you get back alive, you'll have another shot."

"Got it! Securing escape route! **Lumina!**"

Oliver was already moving, aiming his athame over his shoulder and dashing through the shadowless zone with Yuri and Nanao hot on his heels. Lesedi brought up the rear, keeping the zahhak back with her spells. Once they'd gained enough distance, all four leaped aboard their brooms. As they flew off, she glanced over her shoulder at the zahhak swiftly retreating to the rear.

"That counterattack was worse than we'd estimated. Could mean the other squads—?"

"Yo, yo, what the hell?!"

Tim paused in the middle of pulling out his next poison vial. Before their eyes, the still-standing bone knights were grouping around the central general—and combining. Leaving the powerful legs of the skeletal horses as is, countless other bones reassembled into a seat, on which rested the upper body of the general, the rest of his bones built in. The long bone blades on the sides were designed to cut down foes diving to the sides as it charged in. They'd gone from cavalry to nightmarish chariot.

"I take my eyes off you for five seconds, and you get all weird! This makes no sense… Undead are absolute crap at learning new tricks!"

"GYUAAAAAAAAAAAAAAAAAAAAA!"

The general roared, and the chariot rocketed forward. Marco stepped out in front of Katie, Guy, and Pete, but even in armor, a troll couldn't soak this charge without injury. The griffin Lyla swooped in, but the general fended her off with its halberd. This was too much for the third-years to handle, so Tim shot out ahead, trying to draw the foe's ire.

"Magnus Clypeus!"

A spell from one side hit the ground in front of them, generating a rock mountain that stopped the chariot's charge. Surprised, Tim spun around—and found a seventh-year, athame in hand.

"…A regulated vengeful horde? Rivermoore's been plumbing the depths of necromancy, I see."

Gwyn Sherwood's voice was soft and calm. Four more students emerged before him, making a beeline toward Katie's group.

"Is everyone okay?"

"Chela?!"

Katie's face lit up. Chela, Stacy, and Fay were moving with Shannon Sherwood. Shannon was hardly a fighter, so this squad had both her and Gwyn as supervisors.

"Huh?" Tim said, baffled by the reinforcements. "Why are you over here? The rendezvous isn't till later."

"Seemed wise to do so sooner. Too many unfamiliar noises here."

Gwyn answered succinctly, casting further spells to keep the chariot pinned down. Meanwhile, Shannon took a position in front of the younger crowd.

"…Stay…behind me. Don't worry… I'll protect you."

"No, thank you."

Stacy and Fay stepped right around her. Athame at the ready, Stacy glared at their foe.

"I appreciate the supervision, but we're not asking for protection. We have the numbers now. And I'm done listening to this racket. Let's silence it for good."

Her manservant smiled at that.

"Fay," she said. "Run circles around it. Chela and I will hit it hard."

"Got it."

Stacy raised her athame high and chanted a spell.

"Lunatum."

A pale light appeared above her, shaped like a crescent moon. As the spell took effect, Fay's body began to change. The bones in his lower half creaked, sharp claws pierced his boots, his hair stood on end, and fangs appeared beneath bared lips—but there, the transformation stopped. By design.

"...*Hrffffff*..."

Partially transformed, Fay took several deep breaths.

"Phased transformation on a werewolf," Tim said, impressed. "I was shocked by that in the match, but seen up close, I seriously can't believe it. And you can still cast spells? Pretty sure there's no precedent for *that*."

"...Aren't you in pain, Mr. Willock?" Chela asked.

Fay grinned, his features significantly wilder than usual.

"I absolutely am. But my pride outdoes that. That's what loyal guard dogs are like, Ms. McFarlane."

He made his feelings clear in a way that brooked no argument. Chela nodded and joined them.

Gwyn snorted. "No point in trying to stop you. Fine—let's take this thing down. But don't get too far ahead. Shannon'll cry if any of you up and die on us."

He phrased it to sound like a joke, but his expression made it clear it wasn't one. Chela, Stacy, and Fay glanced her way and saw that Gwyn spoke the truth—Shannon indeed looked ready to cry already.

"Don't...be rash...," she said.

"Oh… Argh, fine! Point taken!" Stacy gave up, promising, "We'll play it safe!"

As she did, Fay kicked the ground, his legs far stronger in this form. He now had the mobility to kite the chariot around, and that got Katie, Guy, and Pete motivated again.

"Can't let them hog all the glory, can we?" said Guy. "What do we do about this big fella?"

"Whatever we can, but don't put too much burden on Marco and Lyla. They're already hurt enough."

"Unh? I fine, Katie."

"KYOOOOOOOOOOOOOOOOOOOO!"

Marco offered reassurance and Lyla a powerful howl. Tim grinned and grabbed an extra-large poison vial.

"Guess we're all in! Let's get our murder on!"

After abandoning the battle against the modified zahhak, Lesedi's group spent a solid ten minutes flying around.

Worried this was a bit too bold a move, Oliver asked, "Is this okay? We've been flying awhile."

"Yeah, he already knows we're here," Lesedi said. "Rather than try and hide ourselves down below, we might as well get the lay of the land. Seems like a lot's changed since I was last here."

Given the scale of the place, exploring on foot would take absolutely ages—her reasoning was sound. Oliver was more concerned about their foe's preparations. He found it hard to believe the warlock had no antiair plans.

As Oliver scanned the air around them, Nanao's focus lay elsewhere— on the broom between her legs.

"…Amatsukaze's gait is a shadow of itself," she said. "The air here isn't right."

"Exactly." Lesedi nodded. Then she added, "Lots of magic particles around, but they tend to stagnate. Good for the undead, bad for us and brooms. Watch the drain on your mana and energy."

Her instructions were simple and apt, her answers clear and swift, and above all, she insisted on retreat and survival—there was no doubt she made an excellent supervisor. That was why all three could trust her to steer their course.

"But even with that in mind, the maneuverability brooms provide is effective here. The undead don't have brooms. Only a handful of Rivermoore's bone beasts can match this flight speed. Long as we watch out for them..."

Even as she expounded on the basis of this flight, she trailed off. The others soon figured out why. There were three things up ahead, flying at their altitude.

"Speaking of... We got undead wyverns incoming. Time for a magic flight combat lesson!"

With that pronouncement, Lesedi shot forward, the others close behind. It was their first time going up against wyverns in the air, but they knew the basics. First, don't get hit by their breath—that might kill you outright. Second, don't let that worry you so much that you slow your flight speed. Even without clubs, even against the undead, the key principle of aerial combat remained unchanged. Maneuver yourself above your foe, and victory was yours. And it helped that they outnumbered the enemy.

Neither side seemed inclined to give way, so it started as a bullfight. A vital moment that would set the standings. The wyverns tried knocking them down with claws or their breath while the mages made minimal adjustments to avoid that and fired counterspells, aiming not at the rock-solid bodies but at the more pierceable wings. Lesedi knew that theory well, leading them right at the head wyvern—

"Hng?!"

She'd dodged its jaws easily, but a blade swung at her from the wyvern's back. She got her athame up to shield herself, but the pushback was enough to make her flight line wobble. As the other wyverns shot past, Oliver gulped.

"Ms. Ingwe!" he yelled.

"You okay there?" Yuri asked.

"...Rrrgh. I'm fine! Keep your eyes on 'em!"

Lesedi soon got her broom under control, but there was no time for relief. They'd spotted the source of that surprise attack—a six-armed, three-faced bone warrior, mounted on the lead wyvern's back, wielding a giant glaive.

""""SYURAAAAAAAAAAAAAAAAAAAAA!""""

With a guttural roar, the wyverns came out of their plunge, banking upward. Shooting them a sidelong glance, Lesedi growled, "An undead dragoon? Damn it, Rivermoore, how many more headaches you got up your sleeve?"

"My moment arrives!" Nanao cried, spying her task and upping her broom's speed.

"Wait, Hibiya!" Lesedi cried. "Playing to our foe's strengths won't—"

"Let her do it, Ms. Ingwe," Oliver said. "The sky belongs to *her*."

Catching his point, Lesedi glanced at the ground. Flat land, few elevation shifts—if they took the fight below, there was little chance of using the terrain to their advantage.

"A pain either way... Fine, Hibiya, that dragoon is all yours! Horn, maintain speed and watch Hibiya like a hawk! Leik, you and I are on the other bone dragons! Take them down fast so they can't disrupt Hibiya's duel!"

"On it!"

"Hell yeah!"

The plan set, all four sped off. Gaining altitude and going into a turn, Lesedi and Yuri fired spells at the unencumbered wyverns, drawing their attention. The creatures gave chase, leaving Nanao free to take on the dragoon one-on-one. But before their second clash, black smoke began leaking from the wyvern's jawbones.

"Hrm!"

Spotting the warm-up to a breath attack, Nanao pulled hard to the lower left. The wyvern's jaws opened, and it belched a pitch-black smog, polluting the air. To the rear, Oliver gulped. Being undead, the breath's element did not match that of a living wyvern, but bathing in it would prove equally deadly. Nanao enhanced her katana with the oppositional element, negating what smog she couldn't dodge—

""""SYURAAAAAAAAAAAAAAAAAAA!""""

—and in that moment, the dragoon swung its massive glaive through the mask of smog. Nanao leaned out of the way and was through the clash. Feeling the sting of the smog on her skin, she snorted.

"That breath *is* a nuisance. How might I turn the tables here?"

It wouldn't be easy. Turning to avoid the breath was too large a disruption to her flight path and inevitably slowed her momentum. She could stifle it with the oppositional element, but plunging directly into the breath would leave her exposed to the dragoon's glaive in poor visibility. Defending against two attacks with one katana was no trifling matter, and she was still considering her options as each completed their turn, heading into the next clash.

"Phew!"

On the approach, another billowing breath. Stifling that, Nanao turned downward, going under the wyvern, assuming that given where the dragoon was mounted, no swing of its glaive could reach her. Yet—

""""SYURAAA!""""

—as the veil of smog parted, she found herself face-to-face with the dragoon, mounted upside down, its glaive coming straight at her. A snap of her katana deflected the strike, but the jolt had a significant impact on her speed. Her opponent had done a 180-degree roll to match her position, and as she evened out her path, Nanao couldn't help but be impressed.

"You predicted my move? This will not be so simple!"

"Don't rush the outcome!" Lesedi roared. "That's a bad habit, Hibiya! Remember, you've got backup with you!"

That made Nanao reconsider her strategy.

"Point taken. That was exceedingly rash," she murmured.

A swift dispatch, freeing her up to assist others—years fighting outnumbered in a doomed war back home had left that attitude ingrained. But that was not needed here. She had reliable comrades, and their help would lead her to victory.

"In which case, I shall end it in *three*."

She cast off the unconscious shackles, focusing on gaining speed for the next exchange.

"...Yes, Nanao. That's it," Oliver muttered, watching from above, seeing her fight the way she ought to. "Don't make this about reading each other's next move and snatching victory from those slim margins. You never once needed that. This is your sky, and you're faster than *anyone*."

What she did next was much as he'd imagined it. After the second clash, she opened up the throttle and turned part of her speed advantage into altitude. And with that behind her, Nanao slashed at the dragoon from above—the exact opposite of her last approach, and for a very simple reason. At this height, the wyvern couldn't aim its breath higher; if it rolled to do so, the glaive wouldn't reach.

"SYURAAAAAAAAAAAAAAAA!"

The speed advantage was too great for it to handle a head-on rush. Sensing that, the dragoon dropped the glaive and pulled new weapons from its hips, one in each of its six limbs. The blades were dramatically curved—these were harpes, hardly designed for jousting. The dragoon's goal here was to pull Nanao into a mutually assured destruction. But—

"Impetus!"

—even with blades brandished before her, Nanao wreathed the wind around her own blade, sweeping them all aside. Her slice went through the dragoon's spine to the wyvern's, sending both rider and mount plunging to the ground below.

"Nice! Let's finish off the others!" Lesedi yelled.

Nanao had taken out the real threat, and now they could double up on each of the remaining wyverns. This proved little challenge, and no sooner were they downed than Lesedi put her broom into a dive toward the ground below.

"Mm? Descending now?" Yuri asked.

"The dragoon's got me curious. Like that shadow manipulator, it goes against standard necromancy. Might learn something from the remains."

Back on solid ground at last, they found the downed dragoon on its crumpled mount, a silent heap of bones. But Lesedi approached with caution, athame at the ready. Nanao had cut the rider free of the wyvern, but part of that six-armed, three-faced soldier was still moving, harpe in hand, despite the incomplete skeleton. Lesedi swiftly kicked it apart and made observations on the remains.

"...Yeah, it wasn't just *riding*. The dragoon's bones were fused with the wyvern's at the back. Reminds me of Ophelia's chimeras."

The younger students mulled that over. The rider hadn't been mounted—more like it had *sprouted*, growing directly from the wyvern's spine. No such creature could exist in the natural order of things.

"...Uh..."

Lesedi had been taking the wyvern half apart, but once she got to where the heart would be, she found a bizarre bony lump. She split it open with her athame and revealed a shard of bone within, the size of a pinkie. Hefting it with her wand, she had the rest of the group take a closer look.

"...Not a wyvern bone or a zahhak's," she said. "Clearly human and relatively new. Gotta assume it's the core of some spell."

"A human bone? Then—"

"Sadly, not the piece Godfrey's missing. The mana signature feels familiar. I suspect this is Rivermoore's *own* bone. But how this functioned, I can't say."

After a few more observations, she wrapped the bone in insulation paper and pocketed it. None of them was well versed in necromancy so they couldn't exactly do a deeper analysis on the spot.

Putting it out of her mind, Lesedi told the group, "Either way, too many fights in rapid succession. Fatigue affects your battle performance, so rest is key. Other squads will have secured bases; let's head to one of those."

Regaining stealth, they proceeded on foot a good two hours before reaching the frontline base. Through the well-camouflaged entrance, a path led down, and inside they found the bulk of a familiar troll.

"Marco! Keeping guard, are you?"

"Katie must've summoned him. You're not hurt, are you, Marco?"

"Mm. Nanao, Oliver. Glad you safe."

The two gave Marco a hug as they spoke. Hearing footsteps rushing over, Oliver turned—just as Shannon clung to him.

"Noll!"

"S-Sis... Really, don't do this in front of people."

"Hmm...so it's okay in private," came a voice as frosty as Shannon's was warm.

Making no move to fend off his cousin, Oliver looked around—and found a curly-haired girl, arms crossed, glaring at him.

"Katie..."

"Nanao, Mr. Leik, Ms. Ingwe, welcome. There's tea brewing, but none for Oliver. He already has his hands full."

With that, she pursed her lips, pointedly turned away, and stormed off. Oliver went limp in his cousin's arms, and three other friends took Katie's place.

"Don't worry—she's putting your cup on, too," Guy assured him.

"Guy, Chela, Pete..."

"Her compulsion to compete with Ms. Sherwood baffles us all. When she's done so much for Katie..."

Chela shook her head, and Pete shrugged, snorting. Oliver was now vainly struggling to peel himself away—and Lesedi grabbed his shoulder.

"Horn, one extra rule just for you. Don't bring your love life onto the battleground. Hear me? You're digging up a bunch of memories I'd rather leave buried, and it's making me wanna puke."

"I-I'll bear it in mind..."

She clearly had history with this, and her glare was so intense, he could only nod. At that point, Shannon finally released him, and they were led into the break room. Plain chairs and tables—and at the back, the Toxic Gasser was sipping his tea.

"'Sup, Team Horn plus one. Looks like nobody died?"

"Who you calling 'plus one'? I ain't letting anyone die on my watch. You didn't accidentally poison any of yours, right?"

"I did not. It's such a pain in the ass! Their toxin resistances are total garbage. Most Watch members can inhale a fume or two, but these kids? Nooope."

"Nobody wanted it that way anyhow."

Their standard-issue banter. Lesedi took a seat, and her team settled in, too. Oliver glanced around the room and saw Stacy to one side, avidly performing a physical exam on a shirtless Fay. He waved a hand at them, and they responded in kind.

Soon enough, Katie had tea for everyone, and Guy plonked a plate of cakes in the middle of the table. Oliver was relieved to find there *was* a cup for him. Once everyone had refreshed themselves, Lesedi put down her cup.

"Okay, let's trade intel. We've brought back a broad grasp of the land and combat with a zahhak and an undead dragoon, both results of mystery meddling. The latter we took down, recovering what seems to be one of Rivermoore's own bones from the remains—"

"Then you chickened out and ran from the other?" Tim cut in.

"I *will* kill you."

"I'm kidding. We got kids with us; can't take the risk. We were much the same. Two squads together took out a big-ass ghoul and secured a similar bone fragment. I thought it was the same thing I'd fought in the past at first, but it transformed into something else halfway. Aalto's familiars and Mr. Willock really pulled their weight in that fight."

"Oh-ho!"

"They did?"

Nanao and Oliver looked to Katie, but she refused to meet their eyes—possibly stewing over what she'd said earlier. They moved on to the other person mentioned, but Stacy was yanking his wrist, pulling him back down.

"Don't move, Fay! I'm not done with the exam!"

"You've examined everything twice, Stace. Let me get dressed."

Oliver grinned at the display, but Lesedi was already back to business. She and Tim unwrapped the insulating paper, placing the two bone fragments on the table and scowling down at them.

"These are definitely bugging me. Rivermoore stealing bones was just his thing, but I never heard of anyone finding pieces of him in his familiars before," said Lesedi. "Might be a clue to figuring out his motives and hiding spot."

"I thought the same, but no one here's much use at reverse engineering necromancy spell components. Was there anyone on the other teams?" Tim asked.

Lesedi frowned, thinking—and Shannon quietly rose to her feet.

"May...I see those?"

"Mm? Think you can get anything from 'em, Shannon?"

Lesedi slid the bones down the table. Shannon came closer, touched her finger to them, and closed her eyes.

"...Mm... Got it..."

Most people present did not know what this meant. But Oliver did. If anyone could glean a clue directly from the bones themselves, it was Shannon.

"...I'll share. Wands together...if you wish to know..."

Her eyes half-lidded, she held out her white wand, and though uncertain, the others placed theirs on it. Oliver among them.

"......!"

In that moment, all five of his senses were overwhelmed by a powerful vision.

Clear fall skies. A quiet coast, the beach running as far as the eye could see.

That alone would make for a pleasant walk. But each step taken made his feet sink deeper into the sand. Ever vigilant against loss of balance, he pressed on, walking like a laden mountaineer.

"Yeah, this is the life! A nice stroll along the shore. The pleasant lapping of the waves, the breeze on your face, the seashells sparkling in the sun!"

"...Agreed, but not when I'm carrying a stupid-heavy coffin on my back."

The girl's voice bright and cheery, the boy's gasped between heavy breaths. The coffin he carried was taller than him, this ordeal all the fault of his burden.

"Now, now, Cyrus, keep those eyes up! Back straight! If you stare at your feet, I can't see anything! The blue of the ocean requires the blue of the skies above; I don't make the rules."

His burden shared his sight and complained accordingly. This seemed unfair, and the boy scowled.

"All this *and* I gotta straighten up...? Are you sure you haven't already turned evil?"

"Ah-ha-ha-ha! I actually have! I'm an evil ghost haunting you, Cyrus! You're on to my game, but too late—your back is already my permanent seat!"

Her voice cried out in triumph, and the boy continued carrying her on along the shore. It *was* far too late to complain. This burden was his to bear.

*   *   *

"Hark at this, then. It'll be your coffin, Cyrus."

That was the day. Light streaming in the windows lit upon the sides of a coffin, before which stood a burly old-timer and a boy who barely batted an eye at the dire proclamation.

"...I know it well, Great-Grandfather. You've always had it with you."

"Gah-ha-ha-ha! That I did. But the spiel needs to be said. Each coffin must always have a bearer; that is our way. I entrust this one to you, my great-grandson. I carried it a long time, but age has caught up with me. My back's not what it once was."

The old-timer slapped his back. The boy found it hard to believe the old ox could be that feeble, but he dared not say so. His great-grandfather patted the coffin's side.

"Your duty, first and foremost, is to keep it safe. And more than anything—to release what lies within. I never managed the second, much to my chagrin."

He spoke with great regret. Surprised at the depth of it, the boy nodded gravely.

"I'm familiar with the Rivermoore calling. But if this one is to be mine, then what are those?"

He looked beyond his inheritance to the back wall, where more coffins stood. The light left the old man's eyes.

"Curious? Then go on...touch them."

The boy did as he was told. Moving closer, he placed his palm on one.

"From the roots the mold around my hands cracking cracking cracking crying shut up go away you're twisting my heart it hurts it hurts where are my legs my legs please bring the breeze please the dust is anyone there—?"

The words came flooding up his fingers like a string of curses. He snatched his hand away like he'd touched hot steel.

"...Ngh...!"

"You heard, then. The insides of those coffins have gone bad. We're saying prayers to console them, but there's nothing to be gained by opening them now. When I said, 'keep it safe,' I meant do anything you can to keep her from ending up like them."

The boy swallowed hard. The old man beckoned him back to *his* coffin.

"The connection's been made. Hand on the coffin and make your acquaintance. She's been waiting for you."

Up close, it looked no different from that other coffin. The boy wasn't looking forward to this, but no necromancer could fear the dead. His mind made up, he reached out—

"Finallyyyyyyyyyyyyyyyyyyyyyyyyyyyyyyyyyyy!"

—and the voice he heard betrayed his every expectation.

"You are so, so, so, so slow! I've been waiting foreeeeeeever! I was starting to wonder if your whole clan had up and died on me! You don't wanna scare the dead, buster. Or you might just kick-start the countdown to crazy ghost town!"

She didn't even take a breath. This was nothing like the curses and wailings so common to the undead—she was just a chatterbox. That was his first impression and one she never shook him of.

"Either way, you're the one hauling—I mean, protecting me this go-around? I know all about you, Cyrus. I saw everything through Douglas's eyes," the voice said. "I'm Fau. I used to have a lot more titles and things, but they don't matter anymore, so best we just keep it simple. I'm so glad I finally get to talk to you! Not that you've said anything yet!"

With that, she added, "Okay, we've got a lot to go over, but lemme say the most important thing up front. I *love* taking walks! So you're gonna love it, too! Better start training those leg muscles now!"

Her declaration rang out loud and clear. And thus, the boy forged a bond with the coffin he would shoulder through the years.

*　　*　　*

"Was that…?"

The memory complete, all eyes blinked open, and Lesedi gave her neighbor a shocked look.

"Rivermoore's memories? How—? You read them from the bone, Shannon?"

Shannon nodded faintly, and her brother, Gwyn, stepped in to explain.

"The logic's simple. Just as Godfrey lost a chunk of his ether along with the bone, Rivermoore's bone has a piece of his ether attached. And the ether is a cluster of information. Shannon can read that—basically a higher form of séances or possession."

"…Damn," Tim said. "It's one thing with a ghost who has the whole etheric body, but getting all that from a tiny scrap with no mind to speak of? What kind of etheric abilities are we dealing with here…?"

He was glancing back and forth between Shannon and the bone, but Lesedi was already folding her arms.

"Well, it's a windfall either way. That memory's likely connected to the heart of his sorcery. Not something he'd readily tell an outsider, anyway. And the old man he was speaking to—pretty sure that was Douglas Rivermoore. Not all that long ago, he failed his two-century passage and perished."

She muttered to herself a moment, then put the thought aside.

"Biggest mystery here is the coffin Rivermoore's great-grandfather entrusted to him. Whatever that thing is, it's clearly the root of all his actions."

"Was that an undead?" Yuri asked. "She seemed super bubbly."

"It's not unheard of," Tim said. "Rare to have them be that clear and conscious, but he was also told to make sure she didn't lose herself. The question is: Whose ghost is she?"

Lesedi snorted. "We don't know enough to say, but if we learn more, we might start to see the shape of things. We can glean information from his bones, and the strongest undead out there have those fragments. Which means..."

"If we keep hunting the toughest undead, what we learn will bring us closer to him. That makes our purpose clear," Chela summed up.

"There's still a possibility of false info clouding the picture." Lesedi rubbed her chin. "But given how unorthodox Shannon's approach is, gotta say it ain't likely. And getting to him through the stronger undead was *always* the plan. So that settles it," Lesedi said. "Focus on taking out the toughest he's got, and make sure you bring back the bones inside 'em. Send out your familiars and let the other squads know!"

The mages sprang into action, certain these steps would bring them closer to their quarry.

CHAPTER 3

A Boy and His Coffin

"Ugh, 'ow *dull*. Where is the fun, eh?!"

In an underground base in a corner of the undead kingdom (turned topsy-turvy from the invasion), his teammates sat around a fire—while Rossi deftly exhibited a one-handed handstand, grumbling all the while.

"I was against the job itself, but I thought at least we could 'ave a decent fight against Rivermoore's undead, no? Yet, the gate guard was the only shot we 'ad! After that, it was all, 'If you see a strong undead, do not fight. Just run.' 'ow am I supposed to 'ave a good time 'ere?!"

"…The emphasis is not on the search itself but on delaying the Watch's efforts," Andrews said, studiously adding tea to the pot he'd brought with him. "Reducing the undead's numbers makes their task easier, so us leaving them be is only logical."

Across from him, Albright took a big bite of fried bacon.

"Count yourself lucky we haven't been asked to directly interfere yet. Worst-case scenario would be going up against Team Horn before the finals."

"Ugh, I would absolutely boycott *that*."

Rossi had moved on from the handstand and was now standing on his head. He began spinning like a top.

His eyes on the leaves unfurling in the hot water, Andrews murmured, "Even if interference is our goal, we're on the back foot. I imagine there are steps being taken behind our backs. Though it's easy enough to imagine what."

*   *   *

Meanwhile, an upperclassman was about to enact one of the schemes Andrews had predicted.

"Haaa-ha. Here we go. Yo! You there!"

Hundreds of skelebirds wheeled overhead. Paying them no heed and giving them free rein, Khiirgi Albschuch of the old student council faction addressed the shadows the creatures cast. Not long after, a gaunt, faceless figure rose up before her, radiating hostility: the same zahhak Oliver's team had fought. Though it was poised to lunge at her, Khiirgi just waved a hand.

"Not here to fight. Connect me to Rivermoore for a minute."

There was a few seconds' silence; then an answer emerged from the zahhak—from the mage controlling it.

"What do *you* want, Alp?"

"Now, now, Rivermoore! Don't be such a wet blanket. I'm here to *help*."

Grinning wildly, Khiirgi stalked forward, her face right up against the zahhak's vortex, as if the warlock's face lay within that whorl.

"This theft of Godfrey's bone. Leo's furious—you ruined his fun! A sentiment I do not share. I mean, this gives us a huge election advantage. I'm almost grateful!"

"Then scram. I'm not inclined to waste units monitoring *you*."

"Haaaa-ha. So you *are* running short."

Khiirgi let out a peal of breathy laughter. Rivermoore clearly had his hands full dealing with all the forces here solo. Thus, her proposal.

"Good news. There's a big pawn right here. And several lively little ones, too. Why not make use of them?"

"This already? You never betray expectations."

"Now, now, you could have suggested it yourself! Our interests are aligned. You wish to use Godfrey's bone for something, and we don't want anyone getting it back. Why would we *not* cooperate?"

Khiirgi acted like the answer was foreordained, but Rivermoore just snorted.

"Like your interference needs my permission. You're going to fight each other either way."

"So dismissive! Even if our approach is the same, having you backing our plays will make all the difference. At the very least, remove us from your undead's hit list. Better still, work *with* us. Think what we could do with this lovely zahhak on our side!"

Her gaze ran across the familiar's body, soaking it in. The undead flinched, taking a step back.

"You think I want *help* at this stage?" Rivermoore sneered. "If you had any real intention of negotiating, you'd send the Barman. You're not worth speaking to."

"Fine, fine," Khiirgi said, throwing in the towel. She tried a new tack. "But you know full well refusing our help will change little. You're going to leave this beauty on me like glue, aren't you?"

She had never expected him to be amenable, nor did she need him to be.

"If you see our backs and the Watch's running from you, you know which to strike down first. I don't even need your promise. I *trust* you, Rivermoore."

"The word least suited to your character, Alp."

And with that, Rivermoore's presence faded. The zahhak sank back into the shadow…and the elf moved on to her next task.

*

While the two forces scraped away at each other in the labyrinth below, a new fight was getting underway on the campus above.

"…*Hahhhhhhhhhhhhh…*"

In one of the combat-league team rooms, Alvin Godfrey was quietly focusing his mind. With only minutes left before the fight began, footsteps echoed in the hall, and his teammates burst through the door.

"We're back!"

"How're you doing, Godfrey?"

Tim and Lesedi spoke on top of each other, and Godfrey never even glanced their way.

"Effective mana output's approximately one-twentieth my norm," he said. "Can't keep anything above a doublecant under control. Each time I cast a spell, pain shoots up from the etheric wound."

"So…?" Lesedi urged a conclusion.

Godfrey's grin was indomitable.

"I'm in peak condition. Let's go!"

""Hell yeah!""

At their rallying cry, the covering on the painting in back was torn away, revealing a forested landscape. The Watch command leaped right on in.

"Here it is, the sixth- and seventh-year combat-league main round! The fourth- and fifth-years were already well worth the price of admission, but once you hit this level, it's safe to say the contents of the matches themselves are closely guarded trade secrets! We're here for the privilege of seeing what tricks our school's biggest and baddest seniors have kept hidden up their sleeves, and what greater source of joy could there be?!"

Once again, Glenda was on announcer duties and extremely hyped up about it. Staring at the images projected from the crystals, she launched right into match commentary.

"Dulling spells applied half-strength, of course. Our first match is in the forest zone! Who are we watching here? None other than Team Godfrey! I need not tell you they would've been a strong candidate to win the whole league, were it not for that motherf—*ahem*, Mr. Rivermoore's surprise attack on the president, a moment that will live in infamy. Rumor has it those injuries dog him to this day, but how will they affect the outcome here?"

"I can't say, but the man himself is here to win. One look at his face will tell you that."

Eyes on the screen, Garland grinned. This observation didn't require a mastery of craft—every audience member here had the same impression. Neither Godfrey nor his companions showed the slightest hint of weakness.

"It's time I introduced our guests!" Glenda roared. "We couldn't get anyone from the third- to fifth-years, so we've brought in the ultimate in fresh faces, our second-years! What do you make of this match, Mr. Travers? Ms. Echevalria?"

"U-uh, I sure hope Godfrey wins!" Dean Travers spluttered.

They'd invited guests from the second-year teams that had made it through the prelim, but Rita and Teresa were disinclined, leaving Dean in the hot seat, and his nerves were showing.

The long-haired blond beside him snorted. Felicia Echevalria, younger sister of the previous student council's leader, Leoncio.

"She asked for predictions, not your wishes," Felicia shot back. "No disrespect to the president, but he's at a disadvantage here. Regardless of how true the rumors of his injuries are, the mere fact that they exist paints a target on his back."

Her background and beliefs both left her supporting the old council's camp, which naturally led Felicia to be rather down on Godfrey's hopes. Dean didn't miss the spite behind her words, but he merely nodded quietly.

"...Sure. It's gonna be a tough battle. I agree."

"——?" Felicia frowned. She had not expected this response.

Glenda picked up the pace. "With those words of encouragement from our adorable juniors, it's time to get this match going! Get a move on, teams!"

"Hmm."

Spotting something in the brush ahead, Lesedi and her teammates all raised their athames high, casting upward. Moments later, a powerful blast of heat fell upon them, annihilating the surrounding brush and leaving them standing on scorched earth. With the view cleared, they looked up—and found three mages in a treetop.

"There you are, Godfrey."

"No hide-and-seek. We're taking you down here and now."

The match had just begun, and another team was already on their heels. Godfrey's side had hardly given away their position, but their foes were not about to be outdone on combat experience. If they knew their position and those of their allies, that experience was enough to pin down the likely positions of the remaining teams.

The seventh-year male leading the opposition glared down his athame at them, snorting.

"It pains me to see you shackled like this. Godfrey's wounds alone are a fatal blow, but with these rules in play, Linton can use barely any of his poisons. And Lesedi, are you in anything like peak condition? You and Linton just came running back up from the labyrinth depths."

"You talk a lot," Lesedi said. "What happened to 'now'?"

The trio above smirked and started running down the trunk.

"Even weakened, your mouth never stops. Let it be your last rites!"

"Whoa, we're just getting started and already Team Efler's clashing with Team Godfrey! Changing the terrain itself with a triplecant like *that's* normal—sure is a top-year power move! How will the Watch respond?"

"They'll be hard-pressed to do so," Felicia said. "With rumors swirling around his condition, Godfrey and his team will want to play it safe here and eke out a certain victory. This is the last thing they wanted to deal with. Facing teams in peak match condition will expose their current shortcomings and make the target on their backs all the larger."

She glanced at the boy next to her.

"The initial momentum is against them. I'm afraid your wish will not be granted, Mr. Travers."

"...I can't really argue there."

Her sarcasm rolled right off Dean. His eyes on the match ahead of him, he looked almost baffled. This threw Felicia off her stride—she'd read him as the type to take this bait.

"I dunno," he added. "I just can't quite picture them losing."

"Really?"

Unable to dismiss that out of hand, Felicia focused on the match again. The opening motions were just as she'd expected—Godfrey's side was being pressed hard by their opposition.

"Tonitrus!"

"Tenebris!"

Godfrey's spell struck the incoming magic, but outclassed, it barely managed a deflection. Anyone could tell he'd been overpowered. On any other day, this would be unthinkable, and Efler's grin grew downright evil.

"Barely able to manage an oppositional? No sign of your ridiculous output! Impetus!"

"Clypeus!"

Godfrey was on the defense for their next exchange, too. Taking full advantage of their superior might, Efler closed in, sneering.

"Buying time, waiting for your companions to save you? Go right ahead—disgrace yourself in front of everyone!"

Even as he tried to wind Godfrey up, Efler remained levelheaded. To his mind, Godfrey had two ways out of this. Enduring until help could arrive was one; alternately, he'd have to commit hard and charge into sword arts range. Efler was ready to handle either approach. He was especially on guard against a charge through the clashing spells—

"——?!"

—but the reality came from *below* his guard range. As the oppositional spells clashed furiously in the air above, Godfrey came sliding below them, closing the gap at ground level.

*   *   *

"A-a Hero's Charge?! No, that's just a headfirst slide! But that low, there's nothing to hit—"

"Oh, but there is."

The sword arts master cut off Glenda's gut-based commentary and sent an order to the student operating the crystals. The view switched to a close-up of Godfrey's hands at Efler's feet—and the crowd let out a yelp. *He held no athame.*

"He sheathed his blade just before the dive and, with his hands free, grabbed his opponent's ankles," said Garland. "This is *his* game now."

Efler's ankles!

Even as the realization dawned, Godfrey used that handhold to drag himself to the back left. Efler winced. Occupying the polar-opposite direction of his dominant hand—no matter how he swung his athame, it would not reach Godfrey.

"...Gah...! Let go!"

He had to break away. Efler tried to move but instead found himself toppling sideways.

"Huh...?!"

"Stay!"

No sooner had Godfrey knocked the legs out from under him than he was alongside his foe, grappling. Efler tried to prevent it, but when he pressed down with his left hand, it sank into a patch of mud. His eyes went wide.

"Grave Soil?! Without a wand?!"

Efler tried swinging his athame—but Godfrey had a grip on his right arm. The student council president's eyes were inches from his. A shiver ran down his spine.

*   *   *

"H-how is he doing that?" Glenda yelped. "What kind of moves are those?!"

Two hands grabbing, pinned beneath his body, legs wrapped around him—even as she spoke, Godfrey was swiftly robbing his opponent of any and all movement options. As the crowd gaped, Garland explained.

"It's called guard passing. Ground techniques using a combo of balance control and spatial magic to counter an opponent's moves. He's reading each and every effort Mr. Efler makes, turning each mistake into a more dominant position than the last."

"B-but that doesn't make sense! Mr. Godfrey sheathed his athame before entering the grapple, and his hands remain empty! Spatial magic may not require a chant, but the vast majority can't be used without a wand in your dominant hand!"

"But he *has* one. Look close at his palm."

Garland zoomed in further, putting it on-screen. Godfrey's right hand had a tight grip on his foe's arm—but in his hand was a short rod, as long as his hand was wide—far too short to call a *wand*.

"A graspable wand or a palm wand. Short and easily hidden. Secure it to the wrist of your dominant hand and grasp it as needed. Attach it to your palm via the same principle as Sticky Edge, and you need not fear dropping it even when your fingers are extended," Garland explained. "Naturally, it's too short to cast spells with. But if you limit yourself exclusively to spatial magic control, it provides *just* enough. He has both hands free for grappling but still has access to spatial magic. In close-quarters combat, that's like having an entire extra arm."

This was a whole stack of techniques all too far removed from the sword arts the students knew. No one in the audience breathed a word.

"Ground fighting was one of the first components discarded as we refined the practice of sword arts. Ordinarily, we prefer to do something before we can be dragged into a grapple. Arguably, what Mr. Godfrey is doing here is not sword arts at all."

With each word he spoke, Garland marveled that *this* would happen in a match he supervised.

"Since the invention of the concept to our present day, sword arts have been challenged by any number of antitheses. Anti-athameism being the poster child for them. But another group argued the following— if we learned from the ordinaries and took swords in hands, then we should not limit ourselves to those. Spells, swords, punches, and grabs—use everything and anything that may bring us to victory." With that, he added, "They call it magicombat. An entirely different system from sword arts—and another way for mages to fight!"

Ground fights have an ending in mind. A minute of grappling, and Godfrey versus Efler reached that conclusion.

"...Gah...! Grrr...grargh!"

Godfrey's arms were wrapped around Efler's neck from the side, using the collar of his coat to constrict the artery. Well aware he was being choked out, Efler struggled desperately, but his athame hand was locked in place by Godfrey's right leg, leaving only his off hand— and even that was nigh helpless, pinned between Godfrey's chest and his own body. If his legs had been free, perhaps he might have had options, but the previous struggles had left his leg buried to the knee in a patch of Grave Soil. There was little he could do with only a right leg.

"...Y-you bastard...! This isn't how a mage fights...!"

"No. This is how you *fight a mage.* The Watch has learned how to fight *you.*"

Godfrey tightened his arms. He'd been thrashing around on the ground quite a bit more than his foe and was covered in dirt, but that did not look at all strange. Alvin Godfrey had always claimed his victories that way.

"…Tch… Gurgh…!"

The teammate facing Tim couldn't resist turning his way—and the moment he did, his leg went numb. Flinching, he looked down…and saw a little hole in the ground and a scorpion familiar stabbing his limb. He quickly stomped it, but Tim was smirking—he'd prepped that familiar specifically to catch his foe off guard.

"Figured you'd finish him *and* your teammate together? I like that plan, but you really shouldn't have taken your eyes off *me*."

Don't let your foe look away. Lesedi was no more inclined to allow that than Tim. She could tell her foe was itching to pop a spell at Godfrey, but she kept herself too close to allow that.

"Go on, take your wand off me—if you think your skull can survive my kick."

"…Ngh…"

He'd held out, but no help came. Realizing his teammates were locked down and he was about to black out, Efler went for broke.

"Rahhhhh…!"

Grabbing together the pieces of his fading consciousness, he threw it all into one last bit of spatial magic. A burst of flames before his very eyes that scorched his cheeks and filled his nostrils with the scent of his own burning flesh—but Godfrey didn't blink. To his mind, getting his face burned off no longer counted as even a flesh wound.

"Krk—"

His last-ditch effort ended in failure, and Efler went limp. The ring around his neck kicked in, rendering him unconscious just before he was choked out, but the results were identical. Godfrey immediately let him go and turned to the remaining foes—a third of his face covered in charred flesh.

"Now it's three against two," he said. "Let's end this before any other teams arrive."

"You got it, Prez."

"Hmph. I was about to handle mine."

"Burn this into your eyes, mages. That's your student council. That's the Campus Watch!"

A student had risen to her feet in the stands, her sonorous voice echoing over the grounds. Vera Miligan, candidate for the next council president. She was here today not as an invited guest but as a member of the audience.

"President Godfrey is fighting through a severe handicap. If we simply compare their raw strength, every fighter on that field is likely stronger than him now. Yet, think of it this way—is that a first for him?" she asked the crowd. "It is not. He has been fighting against the odds since the day he enrolled at Kimberly. He was a first-year, barely able to control his own fire spells, surrounded by upperclassmen who were veritable monsters. I'm sure you all remember your first day, the fear of being thrown into a cage packed with ferocious beasts."

The witch's words brought back memories. Large or small, every student here had experienced some variation on that emotion. Especially those who knew what Kimberly had been like *before* Godfrey— as Miligan herself did.

"Unable to bear that state of affairs, he put together a neighborhood watch and tried to protect his fellow students. They were but a small candle held up against the winds, and from the very start, the forces arrayed against him were always stronger. The odds stacked against him, every fight a struggle, the bitter losses too many to count, yet each brush with death made him stronger and rallied more to his cause— and brought him ever more powerful opponents. Yet, his stride never once faltered!"

Her speech was carefully phrased and powerfully delivered. But Miligan knew for a fact it contained not one word of exaggeration. She had seen it with her own eyes, even helped on occasion. This witch knew full well the thorny path the Watch had walked. And if she was to sum that all up—

"Do not forget, mages. Their foes have always been stronger. Nevertheless, our Watch fought not for themselves but to protect us all!"

A jolt ran down the spine of everyone in earshot, each individual surprised to find their fists involuntarily clenched.

"...First squad in blew it?"

"Regroup. We still have numbers on our side."

Team Efler was not the only group after Team Godfrey. Like Oliver's match, their opposition had allied against them. Team Efler's job had not been to score a victory but to stay alive until the other teams could arrive. Even down a team, the core principle remained.

But as they ran to rendezvous, a wave of fire hit them from the side. They threw out an oppositional spell, glaring through the flames.

"...That ain't what we agreed on."

Like Team Efler, the students before them had agreed to cooperate until Team Godfrey was down. But their silent protests against this betrayal got them nowhere.

"Mm, yeah. We changed our minds."

"Blame the guys who messed up the opening gambit."

The students on either side were grinning, and the man in the center just shrugged.

"I mean, sure, there's schemes going on beneath it, but this is supposed to be *fun*. And what gets the party going like the dancer center stage?"

✳

"Yeeeep, another bust!"

A mausoleum-like building they'd found somewhere in the kingdom of the dead. They'd made quick work of the undead around it, picked their way through endless traps, and found a back room with a significant-looking coffin placed at the center—but the seventh-year leading Oliver's squad let out a wail of anguish, bending over backward. This was Carmen Agnelli, a necromancer who'd joined the search belatedly.

"The architecture's ancient enough, so I got my hopes up, but there ain't so much as a single clue here. If you're gonna waste our time, you could at least leave us a treasure or two!"

Back arched all the way over, her upside-down eyes looked to her juniors for support. Oliver mustered an awkward smile. Carmen was far goofier than he'd expected a necromancer to be, and he wasn't quite sure how to respond. But after a futile effort, her energy *was* a comfort.

"Nope, nope, he's *trying* to piss us off. Okay, let's make the most of this time—let me give you a necromancy rundown. First, what do we already know?"

As they headed back the way they'd come, Carmen switched to lecture mode. Nanao and Yuri each looked at the other, so Oliver went with a safe answer.

"...It's a discipline adjacent to the study of curses. And one said to have been far more advanced in the past than it is now."

"Good! Especially the second part, since that takes us directly to this place. Do your friends here know *why* necromancy thrived in the past? And by extension, why it isn't a major discipline now?"

Carmen clearly wanted everyone contributing. Nanao and Yuri mulled over the question and gave their best answers.

"...If the dead are returning as monsters," said Nanao, "they were given inadequate rites."

"And there used to be a lot more dead who met that description, I guess?" Yuri ventured. "Famine, wars, etcetera?"

Clearly their best guesses—and Carmen snapped the fingers on each hand.

"Good! Indeed, the dead do need to be put to rest. Necromancy is all about finding practical uses for souls that failed to pass on, whatever the cause."

As she spoke, she pointed a wand at the skull of an undead they'd stomped on their way in, causing it to levitate and making the jaws flap in time with her exposition. While Oliver tried to figure out if this was in bad taste, Carmen cheerily yammered on.

"Even dead, they can still *work*. Plain and simple, ancient necromancy was all about acquisition of labor. Before the magic industrial revolution, that alone was huge. These days, we use demi-humans, but back then, the dead did what goblins and trolls do now. At the peak of the age of necromancy, a nation's power was determined by both the living population—and the dead."

She explained it so well, all paid rapt attention. Each of them imagined what life in those days must have been like.

"Naturally, necrocivilizations had their downsides. The undead are tough to handle at the best of times. Most of the time, they're kept here by negative emotions and, left unchecked, are a threat to the living. That means the necromancer has to settle them down and keep them well and truly bamboozled," Carmen said. "But the longer they're in operation, the harder that gets. Time from death makes the undead unstable and increases the curse energy within. Vengeful spirits become like starving beasts, and if specialized mages don't look after them with care, they'll break free and rampage. And if their minds have frayed enough, they'll soon merge with the undead around them. Do you know what happens when that's left unchecked?"

An answer floated across his mind, so Oliver whispered, "A maelstrom..."

"Exactly. The vast majority of the ancient necrocivilizations reached a certain scale and succumbed to that fate. Like the nation itself was consumed by the spell. Your classic autotoxemia. Logically speaking, if you keep consolation balanced with the population increase, you should be able to keep it under control, but what I've explained here is hardly the only obstacle preventing that, and modern views hold that the risks of using undead labor outweigh the benefits. That's why there's barely any necromancers in the Union."

At that point, she paused to look smug. The fact that she was allowed to study the subject at all proved how talented she was. Then she turned her gaze back to the present, allowing herself a little sarcasm.

"Although, our current system of demi-human labor is not without risks of its own. Heh-heh-heh, a thousand years from now, we may just be listed as yet another historical failure. Let's hope not!"

Yuri gave the ceiling a puzzled frown. "So...the kingdom that used to be here perished in a maelstrom?"

"That is the question. I'd go with no—this feels more like an evacuation point, where they came to escape the catastrophe. You can smell it: the desperate struggle to avoid inevitable doom."

That was a loaded statement. As Carmen wrapped up, they reached the exit and stepped out onto a plain bathed in pale light. She put her hands on her hips, thinking.

"You know...that story about Rivermoore assembling a whole human skeleton surprised me. We're both from necromancer clans, so I've gleaned bits and pieces of what he's working on from one source or another. One of those said he was going around to mage families, collecting the bodies of their unborn babies."

Oliver's breath stopped. That phrase cut him to the quick.

"...Unborn...babies?"

"Yep. Aborted or miscarried, any fetuses that didn't make it to birth. That takes on a pretty unique meaning in necromancy circles. In simple biological terms, they're obviously dead, but in terms of the world order, the souls are classified as *living*. Within the mother, they are not yet alive, so if they perish there, they are not numbered among the dead. I assumed Rivermoore was using them for something..."

Carmen shook her head like it didn't add up. But a few seconds later, she abandoned the thought and turned back to her juniors.

"Still, that's enough lecturing for one day. The other squads might have found more of Rivermoore's bones, so let's swing by the base and—"

Pleasant music interrupted her. They looked around but saw no performers. This was a sound on a broader scale, echoing across the entire kingdom.

"...A piano?"

"Oh, a consolation concert," said Carmen. "Haven't heard this in a while."

She closed her eyes, savoring the performance. The others followed suit, lending their ears.

Elsewhere, Katie was in the base, monitoring their surroundings through her familiars. She, too, heard the concert.

"...What a lovely melody," she said.

"Yes...it is."

This comment startled Katie, who'd been lost in the music. She turned and found Shannon smiling at her. Shannon placed a hand on the curly-haired girl's shoulder, leaning in.

"There are many ways...to console the dead... But music...is one of the best."

"Er, um...then this is Rivermoore playing?"

"Yes. It doesn't work...with recordings. You can't just...play well. You must...put your heart into it. Or the hearts of the dead...will never be comforted."

Katie fell silent, listening intently. There was a delicacy to the tone that made it hard to believe that a terrifying warlock could be involved. It was a deeply sad song. In more peaceful circumstances, she'd have closed her eyes and given herself up to the experience.

"......"

She glanced over and found Shannon's profile, looking extra fragile. When Shannon had put her arms around Oliver, her face had lit up like a flower in bloom. That always sent ripples through Katie's heart. A past she did not know, the weight of time, an inescapable reminder of the deep bond that had given them.

"...Um..."

"Mm?"

Sounds meant to soothe the dead had eased the tension between them, and Katie took that opportunity to pry.

"A-are you and Oliver...always like that?"

Even as the words left her lips, her throat felt parched. She was in no position to be asking this, and she desperately wanted to communicate that she wasn't merely asking out of curiosity. But it was not a question she could keep buried much longer. It had been eating away at her since her first year here.

Whether that urgency came across or not, Shannon never once hesitated. She just returned a sunny smile.

"Yes. He's my...precious cousin. My darling little brother... The apple of my eye."

"......!"

All that answer gave her was the weight of history unknown. The festering inside Katie grew stronger still, but she knew too much shame to let those emotions turn this into an interrogation. Cursing her own careless act, she sought a new topic, ready for an escape.

"But I've...not been a good sister."

"...Huh?"

Shannon's next words, however, were laden with such regret and self-flagellation that Katie couldn't miss them—until that, too, gave way to a smile.

"What makes you...love Noll, Katie?"

"Eaugh?!"

This time, it was Katie who was rattled by the intrusive question. She half rose from her chair, spluttering.

"W-we're friends! Um, like, just..."

She struggled to find the right words. Katie had probed first, so she *had* to answer. Her mind flooded with Oliver's expressions and gestures, and she found the answer faster than she'd thought possible. It all came down to one thing.

"He has...a gentle heart," Katie managed, head down, face red.

"Hee-hee-hee. Then we're the same," Shannon said, as if she'd known the answer all along.

Her hand stroked the girl's curly hair. Katie let out a moan of little meaning.

Guy and Pete were not far off, ears perked so as not to miss a word—and the outcome was a huge relief.

"...My hands are sweating," Guy said. "Katie doesn't know the meaning of half measures."

"Ms. Sherwood's nature salvaged things. I bet she knew we were listening."

Even as Pete spoke, Shannon smiled toward them. Guy winced and sighed.

"Utter defeat. Maybe you'd better go pry a bit yourself."

"No need. Whatever lies between her and Oliver doesn't bother me."

Pete went back to tuning up his scout golem, dismantling it at absurd speeds, inspecting the parts within.

"I'll make him see me. No matter who else he has, that's all that matters."

"Y-yeah?"

Guy blinked at him. Pete finished the inspection and put the golem back together. It sprang to life and landed on his friend's shoulder.

"Yo, we're back," Tim announced. "If you died while we were out, show your hands."

Oliver's team had returned to base that afternoon. That evening, Tim and Lesedi got back from their matchup on campus. The Toxic Gasser's greeting earned a grimace from Chela.

"That's hardly a joke under these circumstances... But I take it you won?"

"'Course. We're the Kimberly Campus Watch." Tim, still in his cute little dress, crossed his arms and snorted haughtily.

"Anything come up while we were gone?" Lesedi asked.

"Five more bone fragments. And Rivermoore himself performed a consolation concert."

Gwyn, too, was using the enchanted music from his viola to soothe everyone's fatigue.

Lesedi nodded. "Our actions have been stirring up the undead. That's a good sign. The more time he's gotta spend managing them, the more wiggle room that gives us."

Her gaze fell on the table before her. Five new bone fragments were placed in front of Gwyn, evenly spaced on a red cloth. All of them had been recovered while she was away.

"Let's see what these tell us. You up for it, Shannon?" she asked.

"Mm."

Shannon nodded and rose to her feet. She moved over to the table and pointed her wand at the bones. Everyone gathered close. Like the others, Oliver placed his wand over his cousin's.

"Necromancy was just *everywhere* back then."

The girl's voice spoke of the distant past. It was one of the few times her relentless cheer subsided.

"For instance, sometimes a family member will die in an accident or from a sudden illness. Those left behind grieve for them. But if they're undead, then you can be with them awhile longer. A lot of factors went into the creation of necrocivilizations, but I think that basic human urge was at the root of that culture."

Fau's coffin on his back, Rivermoore was working through a pile of ritual bones. She'd told him all this before, but he never let it go in one ear and out the other.

"...Did you have anyone like that?" he asked her.

"Mm. A brother and a grandmother. They weren't exposed skeletons or anything! At the time, there were lots of ways to make them look lifelike. At a glance, you couldn't even tell they were dead! Grandma asked to be made prettier than she ever was in life—oh, that was a secret. You didn't hear it from me, Cyrus."

Rivermoore chuckled.

"If you spoke to them, though, you'd know they weren't the same," Fau said. "My brother and grandma were the nicest people, and they were our family whether they were alive or dead. I'll admit, a lot of that was down to where I was born. Mage families often got excused from postmortem labor."

"Postmortem labor?"

"What it sounds like. Once you were dead, they'd put you to work. Can't have a necrocivilization without that idea. One effective means of operating your undead was to place them under contract while they were still alive. That way, you could smoothly put them under control once they'd died," Fau explained. "Basically, all ordinaries had to do that. The length of their labor depended on their contributions to society or criminal records. If you wanted to relax with your family after death or just pass on right away, you'd better work hard in life. Harsh, right?"

The coffin heaved a sigh. Rivermoore lined polished bones up to one side.

"There's no end of flaws or problems with it, but...it wasn't nearly as dystopian as the name makes it sound. There were good things and bad, smiles and tears. That hasn't changed, has it?" Fau asked.

Rivermoore nodded. It occurred to him that if she knew what passed for normal in those societies, part of her life must have been when things were still going well. But if her world had stayed that way, she wouldn't be like this now.

"...Did it crumble overnight?"

"Pretty much. Not *literally* overnight, like in those stories the ordinaries tell. But I sure won't ever forget that maelstrom. It swallowed up three towns, and we burned another five to stop the spread. Tens of thousands must have died—my mother among them."

The girl's voice spoke of her downfall without emotion. She'd likely told the tale countless times, to Rivermoore's great-grandfather and to whoever had carried her before him.

"From there, it was like rolling down a hill. Distrust for necromancy had gone through the roof. Mages betrayed one another at every turn. And the result of all that backstabbing? An anti-necromancy faction seized control. No idea what happened to them after that. By then, we'd already fled to the labyrinth."

"The one beneath Kimberly?"

"Right you are! That's where your ancestors dug me up. I was shocked when I first heard about it! When did they put a school on top of me? But I knew the labyrinth had changed hands several times already, so we'd expected someone to take over after us. We'd hoped it would be our own kids and grandkids, not...this weirdness."

"Why didn't the evacuees make it?"

"It was more like they never even meant to. The place was always designed to be a city of the dead. Necromancers at the time had serious issues trusting the living. They change too fast, turn on you— once exiled from your own homes, it's hard to argue with that sort of grumbling."

"...Did you try to leave anything behind? If survival was no longer the goal—"

Rivermoore knew the answer to his question but asked anyway. Fau giggled.

"You know already, silly. Sorcery! We were buried there to bring the necromancy secrets we'd invented to the distant future—to you. Along with thousands of guardians, their souls under contract."

"Are you one of those?"

"No. I'm one of the secrets."

She was quite insistent on that. He could picture her arms folded, chest puffed out.

"You know magic isn't always something you can just write down in a book. No matter how hard we try to describe it, if the blood-line in question dies out, so many spells can never be re-created. The higher the spell level, the more likely that is. In really extreme cases, a super-hard spell can only be left behind if the caster comes with it."

That was one reason mages formed clans. But sometimes, they had to take a step, well aware it would end their bloodline for good. If, for instance, the society they hailed from had collapsed.

"Like I said, necromancers then had no faith in the living. That's why they tried to solve the problem without passing it down through their blood. The zahhak is one failed attempt. They're dead, so they can no longer chant—but they *can* use some unusual spells, right? That's magic they knew in life, left in their bodies as *function*, not technique. Arguably, that has successfully preserved those spells, but they failed to achieve the real goal—passing them on. The specs were too much, and the zahhaks' minds frayed far faster than ordinary undead do. No zahhak there retains any trace of the character they had in life."

So a highly tuned undead? This adjusted Rivermoore's perceptions of the zahhak, and he made a mental note to examine one himself and figure out their secrets.

"They tried this and that but without any real success. But some things they tried aren't exactly total failures, either. Specifically, me. I'm essentially a time capsule. This coffin was designed to ward off the wear and tear on the mage's etheric body. That's why I can still talk to you. I'm like a freshly deceased undead, all shiny and new. Impressed yet?"

"You've convinced me. That's why you never let your mouth rest in peace."

This was a routine dig, a running gag, and it made her laugh out loud.

"You know it! Only problem is—this alone doesn't accomplish anything. A blabbermouth undead is no better than a dusty old book. If I can't wave a wand and chant a spell, I've got no way of passing necromantic secrets to you. Can't do a thing unless I get a body and get out of this coffin."

A tinge of desperation had crept into her voice. Rivermoore was right there with her. She was like this for a reason, as yet unfulfilled. That alone had remained unchanged for more than a thousand years, more than enough time to make any ghost fret.

"That's the crux of it! This coffin may keep my ether from fraying but only temporarily. Once that lid pops open, all of that'll catch up with me at once. In a matter of minutes, every trace of me will be gone. I won't have time to teach you anything. And solving that problem—"

"Requires a new vessel. A new body for you, constructed from the bones on up."

Rivermoore put his duty into words. He could sense her solemn nod.

"Yes. That is the task that lies before you. There was a second, but Douglas solved that after years of labor. And you have the talent the task demands. My hopes are with you, Cyrus."

"I'll do what I can. Only way I can ever put this loudmouth ghost down."

He fended off the weight of her expectations with his usual banter, knowing full well that would earn him far more trust than any dramatic proclamation. And he was equally sure that she saw right through his efforts.

"That's the spirit! But there's no need to rush. Take your time and prepare well, Cyrus."

"I'd rather rush. Gotta let you see the ocean with your own eyes and stop hauling you around. I'll promise you this—I'm not making you wait another forty years."

Rivermoore spoke with the utmost confidence. And the girl in the coffin responded with a peal of laughter.

"Fwahhhhhhhhhhhhh!"

The old man pursed his lips and blew. Innumerable candles studding the giant three-layer cake like a hedgehog's needles were blown away—along with the cream, the fruit, and the top layer of sponge cake. The sugary debris traced an arc through the air, splattering against the boy and the coffin seated across the table.

"Bwa-ha-ha-ha-ha-ha! See? I blew out all two hundred! All that chanting really hones a mage's lungs!"

"...Happy birthday, Great-Grandpa. I see turning two hundred hasn't slowed you down. If anything, you're even more powerful."

The cream-covered boy said the right things, repressing the urge to wish dotage and death upon his elder. Laughing heartily, the old man said a spell, cleaning all the cake off the boy and his coffin.

"Buck up, Cyrus. You know perfectly well I only play these games out of love!"

"I am aware. You've played them enough."

While the boy wiped down his face, Douglas pulled over the remnants of his cake, tearing off a chunk barehanded. He stuffed it in his mouth, cheeks puffed out like a chipmunk, his lips instantly covered in cream. The boy snorted—was that any way for a bicentenarian to act?

"And I have a question for my beloved great-grandson."

"Ask away."

"Can you get further than I did?" he asked, polishing off the last of the cake.

His tone never once changed. But this question contained no trace of humor. The boy straightened up. The old man had always been like this—no barriers between grim and goofy.

"As the inheritor of our great bloodline, it is my life's sworn duty to do so."

"I ain't looking for rehearsed answers. I'm asking your gut feeling, Cyrus. Your premonition, even."

The query cut deep. Caught in the light of his eyes, the boy wavered a moment, then let himself breathe.

"…The honest truth?"

"Mm."

"Forty years at most, thirty if I'm quick. When they mention the mage named Rivermoore, they'll no longer mean *you*."

The boy had crossed his arms, eyes boring into the old man—the portrait of arrogance. The old-timer threw back his head, laughing, spraying bits of cake across the entire room.

"Bwa-ha-ha-ha-ha-ha! That's the spirit, boy! Excellent, excellent! Then I'll just have to snatch the name back in year forty-one!"

With another explosive burst of laughter, Douglas vaulted to his feet and walked away. He paused once by the boy's side and mussed his hair.

"You made my birthday a grand one! My thanks, Cyrus."

"A message from her," the boy said, sensing the time for conversation was over. The coffin on his back spoke through him to her former bearer. "'Congrats on two hundred years. But don't go putting on airs. You've got more wrinkles, and your hair's gone white, but you're still that same kid inside. I'd suggest living at least another century if you ever want to grow up.'"

The old man weighed each word from the chatterbox ghost and then smirked.

"I do miss how she talks. Just like when I carried her."

With that, he walked on. The boy rose to his feet and turned to watch the old man go. Shoulders so broad it was hard to believe he could ever surpass them—a moment of weakness that he soon forced aside.

"…Cyrus, feel like an all-nighter?" the coffin suggested.

"Sure," the boy said.

He'd never intended to sleep that night. Not until he saw his great-grandfather in the light of dawn, his two-century passage complete.

Douglas Rivermoore left the manor with the boy's parents before sundown. The night ahead would be a long one for any mage. As he whiled away the hours, listening to the extra-chatty coffin, the boy lost track of how many times he checked the clock on the wall.

"Come, Cyrus. Your great-grandfather returns."

A knock on his door at dawn's first light, the outcome already clear. If it was good news, word would not have reached them yet.

"The battle started at six last night and lasted until two this morning. It was a sight to behold."

Shouldering the coffin, the boy followed his mother to the entrance hall, where the body lay in repose. No visible injuries. He looked just as he did when he was stuffing his face with cake. Like his eyes would snap open at any moment and make a jest of it all.

"...Good night, Doug. You fought well," Fau whispered.

The boy still couldn't believe this was real.

The departure of an esteemed predecessor did not halt sorcery's progress. It simply meant the burden his great-grandfather had carried now rested fully on the boy's young shoulders.

After orientation, his life at Kimberly began. In his first year, he made rapid progress delving through the labyrinth, and when his skills were enough to clear the third layer in style, Rivermoore made his way to his destination.

"This is the labyrinth city where you were buried? Hmph. It's in shambles," he said, eyeing the faded remnants of the dead as they shuffled through the ruins.

"Mm, it's really bad," Fau agreed from the coffin on his back. "The buildings and the dead were never meant to last this long. I'd love to free them all, but in this state, I can't do a thing."

"I'll handle them. I could use some pawns."

Rivermoore didn't bat an eye—to a necromancer, doing upkeep on fallow undead was just instinctive. When he started cracking his knuckles, Fau giggled.

"Bold!" she said. "Proclaiming yourself their new ruler? Then I know just the place. Let me show you to the throne room."

"The throne room?"

"Go where all the mausoleums look alike. The core of this place lies beneath. That should save you a little time setting up your workshop."

"Ngh..."

The lengthy memories gave way to acute dizziness, leaving Oliver staggering. The views his cousin had gifted them were far too vivid, and though he knew full well it was all in the past, his mind still struggled to keep sight of that.

As everyone pored over the intel gleaned, Lesedi said, "I think we've got the critical piece. If his workshop's in the original headquarters, then he won't have moved. The place where all the mausoleums look the same—that's where we'll find Rivermoore."

That was obviously the most important piece of information. What she was saying made that clear—their search was drawing to a close.

"Get ready for the final rush. The next consolation concert will be our cue to charge."

"I don't like the way the wind's blowing," Khiirgi commented, slipping back into the base without warning. She joined her juniors around the campfire. Rossi was stubbornly pretending to be asleep, but Andrews started prepping a cup of tea for her.

"Oh?" he started. "I thought you were in no rush to recover the bone."

"Haaa-ha. You don't mince words, Mr. Andrews. You're not wrong, but that's based on the assumption that the Watch won't recover the bone themselves."

She broke off to take a big bite of the dried meat toasting on the fire. Elves generally didn't eat meat, but Khiirgi loved it.

"So they're making headway?" Albright asked.

"Feels like it. I'm not sensing urgency in their movements. If they were still clueless on Rivermoore's location, Lesedi would be taking action. She never could abide being patient."

She spoke like they were intimate. Her smile faded as she stared into the fire—the fire in her eyes not all a reflection.

"In which case, we're the ones in trouble. Time we acted like it."

A glimmer of a grin crept across her face. Andrews paused, on the verge of pouring water over the tea leaves.

"...We headed out?" he asked.

"No, I'll go alone. This one won't be *nice*."

She let that last word hang in the air. Andrews bowed as she left, wondering why she'd only just decided this.

"...The way the muscles move. The way. The muscles. Move."

Outwardly, their search was carrying on just as before—but in fact, the Watch search teams were prepping for the final assault. As each squad busied themselves, Rosé Mistral was facing his current quandary.

"Still fixated on that, Mistral?"

"This the thing Ms. Aalto said yesterday?"

"How can I not be?! My fighting style depends on no one being able to tell us apart!"

Mistral's voice was getting a bit loud. The night before, Katie Aalto had told him how she could distinguish him and his splinters, and he hadn't believed her. Then she'd demonstrated and nailed it every time, leaving him rather rattled.

"Gotta pinpoint the problem first. Splinter construction? Or operation? Go through everything unnatural, see if operating only one at a time improves things. Would love to check that against Aalto's eyes, but then she'd just get even better at spotting them..."

Even as Mistral muttered, he was running his splinters through their paces. Not *just* trying to solve his problems—he had his splinters far away from the base, searching as he experimented. They were past the initial intel sweep stage, but their instructions were to search like always. Best not to let the enemy know your plans.

"Mm? What's that hole...?"

There was a weird round hole in the side of a ruined wall, and he sent his splinter to investigate. There might be an enemy hiding within, but even if there was, the splinter would soak the reprisal. Mistral figured it was better to check than play it safe. He peered inside—

"Boo!"

—and a pale elven face filled his vision.

"___!"

Their eyes met. Before he could even make a sound, his muscles froze. A spell was forced through his vision, corrupting his mind.

The splinters he operated were highly precise. That applied not only to appearances and movements; their sensory organs were every bit as accurate as a real human's. And that hurt him now. If a familiar operating in real time had superlative senses, then spells that took advantage of those senses—like this charm—could also be cast through a familiar. Well aware of his unique familiars, Khiirgi had always planned to use him against their search efforts.

"Mm?"

"What's up, Mistral?"

His teammates sensed something off and called out—but by this point, the charm had taken effect. He waved them off.

"Nothing. An undead almost caught me. Made me jump."

"Be careful, man."

"Not like you can readily make more of your little clones."

"I know, I know…"

Mistral turned his back on his teammates. Even he couldn't tell that he was no longer thinking straight.

Another day passed. By the kingdom's throne, Rivermoore was buried in his work.

"…I know this is a race to the finish, but you could use a break, Cyrus," the coffin said.

"Only the final adjustments remain. Make like the dead and stay still."

He was adjusting the finer points of a magic circle with his wand. This circle filled half the broad stone room, containing ring after ring of letters and diagrams. At the center of it was a cloth-covered body: all the bones Rivermoore had stolen—Godfrey's included—assembled into a human skeleton.

"Even the dead need comfort. Same for the living," Fau told him. "You've been alone too long."

"I've got company. A dead girl who talks more than most of the living."

A remark he allowed himself only because the goal was in sight. Well aware of the stress he kept hidden, Fau sighed.

"This whole domineering act is really settling in. But I guess that's my fault, too. I'm feeling some pangs of guilt right now, you know!"

"Spare me your delusions of grandeur. I can't keep up."

Checking the next section of the circle, Rivermoore paused his hands.

"…The dead grow restless again. These grave robbers insist on distracting me."

He snorted and turned to the far corner, where a piano stood. Performances here reached the entirety of the kingdom.

"Ooh, a consolation concert? Can I make a request?"

"Go ahead. I'm in no mood to be picky."

Rivermoore sat down before the keys. Fau named a tune, and he began to play. She listened closely.

"...Good tone. You've improved, Cyrus."

"I'm glad you have no ear for it. Compared to Hymn and Spellstrings, I sound like a child practicing."

"Perhaps on the technical merits alone, sure. But I like your performances best. They echo in my heart."

Rivermoore snorted and kept playing. A few minutes later, however, his fingers halted.

"...? What's wrong, Cyrus?"

"_____"

A long pause followed. He was syncing his vision up to the familiars on patrol, observing the movements of the forces within his kingdom. There was disjointed movement from every direction, all closing in on one location.

"They know where I am."

He left the piano, his thoughts of soothing the dead abandoned then and there.

"Hurry! Don't give him any time!"

Her juniors in tow, Lesedi shot forward on her broom. The consolation concert had been the starting pistol, and their assault began in earnest. She knew Rivermoore would have spotted them by now, but their success hinged on how little time he had to consider his options.

"We're first in! Don't get cocky! There'll be undead waiting for us!"

"Acknowledged!" Nanao replied.

Oliver's squad had been closer than the others, so they were the first on the scene. Compared to the fakes they'd inspected, this looked like another bit of the wasteland, nothing to distinguish it from the surroundings. But Shannon's powers had already confirmed it was the spot. Only one problem:

"Welcome!"

An elf stood before them on the empty land. Spotting her, the team swiftly let down their brooms, landing a safe distance away. Lesedi took the lead, glaring at Khiirgi where she stood.

"I see you got ahead of us. You been working with Rivermoore?"

"No. This just finally got him on board."

Nanao, Yuri, and Oliver drew their blades. The old council faction and Rivermoore's interests were aligned, so Lesedi's group had planned for this eventuality. Thus far, they'd avoided outright conflict, but at this stage, that could go out the window.

"I'm sure you'd love to proceed, but I'm the guard here," Khiirgi said. "Can you get past me?"

"Have it your way."

Lesedi dashed forward. But as her trajectory crossed Khiirgi's shadow—it reared up.

"Lesedi!" Nanao cried.

"——!"

She took a quick step sideways, just as countless spikes shot upward. A moment later, they were followed by something Oliver had never expected to come out of Khiirgi's shadow: the zahhak they'd fought a few days prior.

"Oh, right, I forgot to tell you. I'm not the only guard. I have a partner."

"You're a good match," Lesedi spat. She retreated, giving her juniors orders. "Take the zahhak for me. I'll handle Khiirgi."

"Got it. Fight plan?" Oliver asked, figuring this wouldn't be like before.

Lesedi considered this a moment.

"Go for the win," she said. "Buying time won't do a lick of good. The other squads are in similar straits."

*   *   *

Oliver's team may have flown in, but not all squads took that approach. Even on brooms, if their team was mostly ground fighters, they kept their flight paths low. Lack of personnel left Tim running both Mistral's and Ames's teams.

"Whoa…!"

"Eh?"

But a burst of fire blocked their trajectory. Tim veered left to avoid it, and both teams followed suit. Twenty yards hence, the mages firing antiair spells emerged—all familiar third-year faces.

"…Team Andrews? I figured you sided with Leoncio. Trying to stop us?" Tim asked.

"That's the gist of it," Andrews said grimly. Rossi and Albright silently drew their athames.

Tim looked them over and snorted. "Obligations have you here, but you don't wanna be. Cool, come at me. We'll free you up real quick."

His athame went up, while his left hand reached for his pouch. Figuring he should put them under gently, he hesitated over the selection—

"*Tonitrus!*"

—and a bolt from behind struck his right arm.

"Ahhh?!"

The athame fell from Tim's hand, and he rolled to the side. A vial from his pouch held between three fingers, he shot a glare at his assailant: Rosé Mistral, athame at the ready—eyes oddly hollow.

"Yo—"

"What the—?"

"Pardon me."

The moment Mistral's teammates yelped, Ames was running in from the side. Her palm hit Mistral's cheek, every ounce of muscle in the blow. Mistral went flying sideways—and light returned to his eyes.

"…? …?! O-owwww!"

"Are you back with us, Mr. Mistral?"

Ames had her athame aimed at Team Andrews, pressing them back and making sure the spell was broken. Mistral was clutching his throbbing cheek.

"Looks like you were under a charm. I wasn't sure of the specific type, so I thought a slap to the cheek would be the swiftest resolution. Was this your doing?" she asked Team Andrews.

Andrews and Rossi glanced at each other.

"...Most likely—"

"Ah, by 'not nice,' she meant this, eh?"

That was enough for Ames to surmise they had not been informed. She glanced briefly away from them, checking the state of the Toxic Gasser's injuries.

"Please step back, Mr. Linton. No time for healing here. Your poisons are far too intense to use without a wand. If that vial shatters, no one here can contain it."

"...Tch...!"

The toxicity of his poisons and his need to protect his juniors were turned against him: exactly what Ames and the others needed to keep the Toxic Gasser sidelined. Ames stepped forward, laying on the pressure, and Mistral—now back in his right mind—joined her with one very red cheek.

"Don't be concerned, Mr. Linton. This is our job."

"Agreed. You did me real dirty there. Left my molars chattering, too!"

Mistral let out an angry howl, and his teammates flanked him. But Albright looked them down with an icy calm.

"You nobodies sure can howl. But I don't imagine six-on-three gives you an advantage."

"That is the question," Ames said. "At the very least, I believe I can handle *you* one-on-one."

"Ha! All right. I'll take that bait."

Albright stepped forward, facing Ames. She flashed a hand sign to

her flunkies, waving them off. While she kept a skilled foe busy, the others could press the numbers advantage. No one else here could handle anyone on Team Andrews solo.

Their plan was obvious to everyone.

"We get the other five," Andrews said. "Who do you want, Rossi?"

"The big man took the cutie, so I 'ave no interest." Rossi shrugged. "Whoever comes for me."

The Team Ames duo fired spells his way—and for the first time since the search began, third-years were fighting each other.

Meanwhile, Team Cornwallis and the Sherwood siblings also found their paths blocked by familiar faces.

"Oh, if it isn't Team Bowles. I got all tense for nothing."

"Hey, hey, hey! That's no way to say hello, Cornwallis. We ain't good enough for ya?"

The first foe to bark was a male third-year, Spencer Howell.

"Is that a surprise?" Stacy asked. "I saw your match. It was such an embarrassment, I thought I was watching a magical comedy show."

"Gah...!"

Marcus Bowles clutched his chest, staggering back. He'd clearly taken plenty of damage before the fight even began, but Gwyn and Shannon had never so much as glanced his way. While Khiirgi may have left Team Andrews to their own devices, Team Bowles came with a proper supervisor.

"We'll handle their chaperone. Your classmates are all yours," Gwyn said.

Nodding to the opposition's upperclassman, they moved away from their juniors.

Chela watched them go with one eye and stepped up to Stacy's side.

"I'm sorry Stace was so harsh, but we are in a hurry. If you try to stop us, we won't be holding back."

"Don't gripe if I bite off a leg or two," Fay said, flashing his fangs.

At that, the sole silent member of Team Bowles—Rodney Quark—held up his hands.

"...If I might offer an excuse—these two don't get along. One's dead serious; the other's a hedonist. If I'm not there to mediate, the team falls apart. And then I got downed first in the league fight."

Rodney made a face like he'd bitten a lemon. Then he fixed Team Cornwallis with a glare, as if all the frustrations of that fight were driving him here.

"If you wanna underestimate us, go ahead. We'll use that against you!"

CHAPTER 4

Rivermoore: A Minister's Duty

"...There they go."

As Rivermoore's concert let fly the opening salvo, the exit from the kingdom to the third layer was defended by several upperclassmen—and Guy's squad. Lesedi's orders prioritized survival rates, and that meant keeping a solid team posted there. Even if the undead swarmed them, they should be able to hold out until help could arrive.

"I hope they're okay," Katie whimpered, pacing back and forth. "Urgh, I wish we could be there..."

"Relax," Guy said, putting his hands on her shoulders. "Our skills are more suited to defense, and we don't know how the assault will go. Securing a retreat path is a vital role."

"Unh, sorry," Marco said, hanging his head. "I too slow..."

"This is *not* your fault, Marco! Thanks for using that big body of yours to keep us all safe! You've been a huge, huge help!"

Katie quickly put her arms around his big leg. Having the troll with them might diminish their mobility, but few things could match his defense. Marco guarding this location meant the front lines could focus on the battle at hand.

"...Win this thing, Oliver," Pete whispered, eyes on the expanse before him. He did not ask his friend to stay safe. On that front, mages simply kept the faith.

"Progressio."

Khiirgi's chant activated the pre-prepped magic circle, and dark-red growths—somewhere between vines and trunks—reached up from the ground, lifting her body skyward. Oliver momentarily feared these were some beast's tentacles, but on closer examination, they were clearly rooted in the soil.

"Uh, are those plants?" Yuri asked incredulously.

"The soil here, though..."

It was difficult to believe. The magic particles here were agreeable to the undead but offered no boon to anything vegetative. Guy's tool plants would not grow, and Oliver had yet to see a single weed growing anywhere in the kingdom.

But the answer to his query came from Lesedi's bountiful knowledge and experience. As she bounded up the vines after Khiirgi, she yelled, "Undead plants?! You clearly love nothing more than defiling elf sorcery, Alp!"

"Haaa-ha! I'm bucking against repression! This has no place in nature, so back home it was forbidden, profane!"

Khiirgi rode the vines higher, cackling, as still more came after Lesedi, as if they had minds of their own. But Lesedi's pursuit was relentless, dodging, parrying, or using them as footholds to propel herself after her quarry.

"But I can't dismiss those stipulations out of hand, either. These unnatural acts *do* turn the elementals against me, and that makes things rather difficult for an elf mage. Yet, I can't help but feel that is also a curse, binding the elf race to that moldy naturism. Are you with me there?"

"Nope. Don't give a shit about your home life!" Lesedi snapped, hurling lightning.

Khiirgi canceled it with the oppositional element, still monologuing.

"Even when I was at home, I was always wondering. Elves have an inherent aptitude for magic, far greater than humans. We lag behind on reproduction and environmental adaptability, but our long lives more than make up for it. So when the ancient wars were fought over domination of this world, why did we lose to *you*?"

"Bad strategies. Inadequate supply lines."

"Haaa-ha! That's what I love about you! But I have another theory. It was not a matter of preparedness—it was their *attitudes* that were lacking. Elves could not match humanity's pursuit of sorcery, lacked the arrogance to trod roughshod over every principle and doctrine. They hesitated to even take a step in that direction! No wonder that fallen god loved them more than humans."

Her speech was taking on a solemn vibe, yet Lesedi was still slicing her way through the onslaught of vines.

"Even the word *Alp* was once used by the ordinaries in one corner of the Union to describe elves in general. They believed we were child-snatching monsters. Was that the result of human propaganda? Or was that based on actual historical events? I don't know the truth, nor do I care, but I loved the idea of an evil elf. As we are now, that notion is more a blessing than an insult."

The fully grown vines had Khiirgi suspended at their apex. She had her hands folded before her chest, like an actor on a stage.

"I am an outcast elf. Drawn to the immoral, beguiled by my desires, I was driven from my home and washed up at Kimberly. My parents lay together, two virtuous elves—yet the product was the devil you see before you. If there is any meaning to that, I'd call it a *sign*. A reminder that our species is trapped in a dead end, in need of guidance to the next evolution."

Her lips twisted. Her sorcery had begun in isolation back home, her path discovered during her wanderings in the world of man.

"Immorality and the profane are my calling! I am an Alp! Khiirgi 'Avarice' Albschuch!"

Khiirgi's undead plants were still growing. New vines cropped up, pushing her and Lesedi higher and higher until the ground beneath was like a veritable tír forest.

"Hrm. They grow as fast as we mow them," noted Nanao.

"Our damage can't keep up with their speed. At this rate—"

Before Oliver could finish, a blade shot out of a vine's shadow, aimed at his back. He spotted it, dodged, and fired a lightning spell to counter, but to no avail. It fled to a different shadow right after the attack. In the last battle, it had used the bone birds above, but now it was using Khiirgi's forest.

"The quantity of shadows is only increasing, and its advantage with them," said Oliver.

"Should we head up, too? I'm pretty good at that stuff," Yuri offered.

"No, ascending could let the zahhak target Ms. Ingwe. We've gotta take it out at ground level."

Bearing both the situation and their role in this fight in mind, Oliver looked at his companions. When he could find no way to proceed, Nanao's and Yuri's instincts often prevailed.

"This is our second battle with this foe. What are your observations?"

"Um, well, doesn't seem like it can stay in the shadows all that long. Ten seconds max?"

"And the traversal between the shadows is hardly swift. No more than walking across the surface at least."

Even as they fought, both had been carefully analyzing their foe. Watching the shadows around him, Oliver nodded.

"Agreed. And I'll add that there seems to be a minimum size requirement on the shadows it passes through. It uses its own shadow to retreat but must use existing shadows to emerge. Which gives us a lead. **Clypeus!**"

Inspiration struck, and Oliver cast a blockade spell, creating a wall not far behind them. As yet, it served no purpose, but that was the plan. Just like Nanao's fight with the dragoon. If their foe could not be beaten in one move, then multiple steps would do.

"Lock a location, find the moment, drive it there. Follow my lead."

"Gladly!"
"On it!"

"Hfff!"

The instant he was in one-step, one-spell range, Albright swung his blade down from on high. Ames thrust forward, aiming for his wrist, but he'd predicted that and shifted his swing to strike her athame. The force behind the blow nearly unbalanced her, and a backslash from below came close—

"*Hahhh—!*"

A blow designed to overpower her guard, but she put her left hand to the blade itself to block it *and* absorbed the momentum, launching herself backward. Albright grunted and abandoned his pursuit. She'd used his strength to right herself, the resulting posture a marked improvement.

"Hmm, you've got some moves," said Albright. "Shrewd use of your shrewish frame."

"Worn out already? Then let's take it down a notch," Ames replied, striking a mid-stance.

Albright snorted. "Your taunts miss their mark. Why should I close in?" With that haughty remark, he raised his athame high in an intimidating stance. "Scamper on in—I'll be here to crush you. Ideal way to handle rodents."

"Hardly, as I shall not scamper."

Returning snark for snark, Ames moved out, her blade searching for a chance to slash the tomcat's throat.

"You 'ave yet to amuse. Try a little 'arder, eh?"

"You did *not* just say that, you li'l prick!"

"Our boss works us like frickin' dogs!"

Ames's teammates were relentlessly swapping places, and Rossi was weathering the storm, looking underwhelmed. He was clearly getting under their skin, but what did he care?

"I suppose it's better than your league match. Fine, I'll play a round."

Rossi abruptly leaned forward. They assumed it was his patented roll and leaped back—but Rossi maintained that unbalanced lean. Yet, this was no lunge, either—he *slid* along the ground, passing between the girls before they could react and tapping their backs with his knuckles.

"Wha...?"

"H-how did he...?!"

"Koutz fencers prance upon land or cloud. I am getting the 'ang of it, no?"

He turned, smirking. The Ames duo came after him again—but theirs was not the only battle raging here. Albright faced one, Rossi two—which meant the remaining three were on Andrews. Although in practice, he was facing more than *twice* that number.

"...Between the corporeal and shadow splinters, eight sure is a crowd," said Andrews.

"No point holding back here," commented one Mistral splinter.

"We'll make it quick!" said another.

From the get-go, they were going all out with the splinters and transformations. Mistral had assumed the fight would hinge on buying time to make the splinters, but to his surprise, Andrews had hung back, watching him work.

Now Andrews glanced around the eight approaching figures—

"**Impetus.**"

"Whoa?!"

"Yikes!"

The gust hit not from the fore but from behind, pushing hard against the Mistrals. Andrews's eyes caught how they moved.

"I see. **Impetus!**"

Before they could even try to dodge, a blade of wind sliced the two corporeal splinters in half. Andrews backed off a step, dodging the counterspells, and glanced over the six remaining foes.

"At this range, shadows won't fool anyone. The corporeals might—but while three of you recovered your footing by adjusting your center of gravity, the splinters righted themselves a beat too late. You should have matched *them*."

"...Not likely."

"And leave ourselves exposed?"

It was easier to distinguish splinters from the real thing on impulsive movements than calculated ones. Andrews had taken advantage of that and left Mistral gnashing his teeth.

"Since you don't want anyone spotting the differences, you have a bad habit of holding off on spell usage till the last second. You had the numbers advantage, yet you let me make the first move. If you've had time to make proper preparations like your previous match, that would be one thing, but—on a chance encounter like this, it's obvious your tricks aren't fully meshing with magic combat."

"Damn, hit us where it hurts."

"You're tearing us a new one!"

With fewer splinters, they changed formations. A momentary shift in focus—and a lightning bolt hit them from the side. They tried to leap back but couldn't fully dodge.

"Gah...!"

"You're a serious man, Mistral," Andrews intoned. "You're paying me too much attention."

Left arm numbed from the bolt, Mistral swore, glaring at the source. Rossi grinned back, having fired a spell between the Ames duo. The two girls quickly backed off, regrouping with Mistral.

"Sorry! Couldn't pin him down!"

"Rossi pisses me the hell off...!"

"Don't worry," Mistral assured them. "I messed up first."

He gritted the teeth Ames's slap had loosened. And he *had* been too focused on Andrews's advice to watch his surroundings. Lots to work on, but he'd have to beat himself up in the postmortem after.

"You don't get to the finals for nothing, huh? But we've had more than our fair share of screwups!"

Mistral raised his athame, whipping up his team's spirits all the while. His teammates and Ames's put their heads in the game.

Watching them all from the back, Tim ground his teeth. With his casting hand down, he couldn't even heal himself. He had a pouch full of poison, and the virulence of it was eating away at him.

"...No poison on hand I can use against kids without a wand. God-damn. I came prepped for the big guy, and it bit me in the ass."

"Awoooooooooo!"

Fay let loose a howl before shooting forward and tackling one of Bowles's teammates. With both legs phased to werewolf form, his speed was fully bestial charge. Spencer barely blocked the blow, but he was nonetheless steadily forced back.

"...Ngh...! You're really going for it, Mr. Willock! I ain't into being on the receiving end of this violence!"

"Funny—I'm the same."

Fay flashed a grin, pressing his animalistic advantage. It looked like a one-sided fight, but from behind, Stacy could tell Spencer was handling things well—he was half *pretending* to be on the ropes, making it look like he was barely blocking, trying to bait Fay into a swing too large.

"...Huh. So you *can* move," Stacy said. "You should have done that in the match."

"We meant to!" Bowles wailed. He swung his athame, and Stacy batted it aside into a counterthrust. Their duel was playing out at one-step, one-spell range, with Chela watching over it from a distance.

"...I see. A pair of aces, with you as the commander. That's your team's true style."

"An honor to be noticed and recognized," Rodney Quark said with a sigh. He was facing Chela at casting range. "If you hear anyone dissing our previous match, maybe drop a word? *They're better than that* would suffice. At this rate, our marriage prospects are slim…"

In the league match, Andrews had spotted his hiding place and taken him out early, giving him no chance to show off.

"That does sound urgent," Chela replied, wincing. "If you can down us here, I promise we'll spread the unvarnished truth. Will that do?"

"Splendidly, Ms. McFarlane. I'm so glad we could come to an agreement."

They abandoned conversation and went back to their spell duel.

Some distance away, the three supervisors were glaring one another down. Team Bowles was overseen by a seventh-year from the old council camp: Elise Cuvier.

"I expected as much, but your sister really doesn't attack," she said to Gwyn. "Is there a constraint upon her, or are you just playing it close to the chest? Which is it, Sherwood siblings?"

"If it was the first, we'd hardly answer. And if it was the second, the answer will only come out if you back us into a corner. Either way, you're wasting your breath, Cuvier."

"So unsporting, Spellstrings. The melodies you play are far more eloquent."

Cuvier's wand wavered, and the first syllable of a spell crossed her tongue. Gwyn's response had already begun. That syllable narrowed down her spell selection, and with decisiveness matched by few even in the upper forms, he could often get a counterspell off first, but—

"*Frigus!*"

—as he focused on the enemy before him, a fireball descended from overhead. Shannon spotted it and canceled it with the oppositional element, but the foe behind that surprise attack was far above. A trio of brooms wheeled in the sky. Gwyn frowned.

"Spells from that height? And accurate despite the brooms' speed, too… Team Liebert?"

"Pretty cool, huh? They caught my eye in that last match. All three are fine, but Ms. Asmus in particular will be an excellent pawn. Let my promising juniors get a taste of victory's nectar."

"Not happening," Gwyn said, dead serious. "We're too busy looking after our own little brother."

Cuvier smirked and aimed her wand.

Team Horn and the zahhak were still battling in the shadow of the undead plants. They chiseled away at each other's nerves, exchanging breathless blows, and at last Oliver spied the moment he'd been waiting for.

"Time to seal the deal, Nanao!"

"Gladly!"

Nanao braced her katana at the hip. On the breath before her chant, Oliver and Yuri leaped together.

"Gladio Ferrum!"

A doublecant severing spell shot beneath the boys' feet, slicing through the trees around like reaping wheat. Their base undone, the unnatural trees began to topple, but since the cuts matched the angle, the direction of that fall was preordained. All three members of Team Horn were soon out of the landing zone, but the zahhak had no need. It simply ducked into its shadow, waiting for the collapse to complete.

"It dove! **Fortis Flamma!**"

"Fortis Flamma!"

Oliver's and Yuri's flames ignited all the fallen trees. Ordinarily, fresh timber didn't make good kindling, but the reversed attributes meant the undead plants went up with a sinister dark-red flame. But what mattered here was not the burning lumber—but that those roiling flames coated the entire area.

"...Fire's blocked every escape route," said Oliver. "Only one place it can go. Only one shadow a yard across it can reach within ten seconds."

The fallen trees were covered in flames, and the zahhak could not escape that way. The wavering flames disrupted the remaining shadows, making Shadow Crawl itself difficult. Under those limited conditions, the zahhak had few choices, and the time limit on the crawl itself meant it could not stop to think.

The zahhak found a shadow within that ten-second range and popped its face out to take a breath. In that one defenseless moment, all three athames bore down.

"Yes, *there.* **Tonitrus!**"

"**Tonitrus!**"

"**Tonitrus!**"

Three bolts all struck home, and the zahhak fell over. They hit it with another round to be sure, but it didn't budge. Certain the beast was felled, Oliver let out a sigh of relief.

The groundwork had paid off, leading their way to victory. Reduce the zahhak's options with the burning trees and lead it to an exit of their own devising. The final shadow it emerged from was beneath the wall Oliver had made with that blockade spell. Their foe assumed it had chosen that spot itself, but they had led it there.

"Yuri, grab the bone fragment. Ms. Ingwe! Ours is down! Expect cover fire from below!"

The fight was still raging up above. Lesedi was almost dancing through the air.

"What, already?" Khiirgi gasped. "That was a pretty powerful creature!"

"And they're the top of their year. Four against one. Wanna beg Rivermoore for more backup?!"

"No, no, I have my own."

Even as she spoke, two more students swooped in on brooms. Seeing Albright and Andrews, Lesedi clenched her jaw.

"Team Andrews? They got through our side, then!"

"I've got good kids on my side, too. Haaa-ha! Four-on-three. More fun to come!"

Khiirgi let out a cry of glee, but Lesedi's voice grew quiet.

"...I've been meaning to tell you something, Khiirgi."

"Mm?"

"You're a powerful mage. One of the top ten fighters in the seventh year. On combat alone, I can still match you, but on the total magic package—you've got me beat."

"My, my! Where's this coming from? You're making me blush. Not often you shower me with compliments."

The elf put her hands on her cheeks, looking bashful.

"Don't get ahead of yourself," Lesedi said. "My point is: You've got a fatal flaw that pulls the rug out from under all your raw talent."

Khiirgi blinked and looked at the juniors around her.

"Oh? My, my, my."

Andrews and Albright grinned. The disguises covering their faces fell away, and the true faces beneath emerged—Mistral's teammates.

"On to us already? Here's a message from our leader."

""Payback's a bitch—and so are you.""

Both fired staggered spells, the first of which Khiirgi canceled with the oppositional element. The second, she dodged with a leap from an undead tree leaf, easily moving herself out of harm's way. But this was mate in five. To avoid the third spell Lesedi fired at her feet, the elf was forced into a Sky Walk.

"This is what avarice gets you."

Lesedi kicked off the undead plant herself, Sky Walking in close. Khiirgi waited till the last second, then double feinted into a second Sky Walked sidestep. Lesedi's kick caught only empty air—or appeared to, but her sole trod firmly on the void. Khiirgi winced, realizing her mistake. She'd already used both Sky Walk steps—but Lesedi had one remaining.

"Get it yet? Your flaw's quite simple. Nobody fucking likes you."

She had her quarry right where she wanted her, and the Hard Knocker went into a spin kick. Khiirgi had no other choice but to use her left arm as a shield, yet Lesedi's kick went through that bone and shattered against the Alp's ribs.

"Success," Mistral muttered upon receiving word from his companions. Andrews and Rossi were still fighting them—but at that, they paused.

"Then our fight is done. Thanks for playing along."

"Ooh, caught that lady unawares, eh? Wish I 'ad been there."

Rossi's spirits immediately soared. He was outright whistling.

"She disgraced me first." Mistral scowled. "And I'm none too pleased about having the opportunity handed to me. Aren't you old-council camp?" he asked Andrews.

"Our families are. But our priority now has to be victory in the combat league. If we're dragged any deeper into the election back fighting, it'll effect our performance."

Andrews was clearly highly annoyed to have been brought here at all. His frown deepened.

"And on a personal basis, I'm against this approach. President Godfrey demonstrated his character in the senior league prelim. That may have allowed Mr. Rivermoore to catch him off guard, but his choices at the start of the match also ensured minimal student casualties. The old council is merely reaping the benefits—and that's a pathetic way to win an election. How can they inspire any kind of following like that?"

Perhaps in his first year—before Richard Andrews met Oliver and Nanao—this would not have occurred to him. But he knew better now. He knew both victory and defeat could be achieved the right way and the wrong way.

"The old council needs to prove themselves. Show us who they are and how they'll lead Kimberly in the future. The best way to do that is to go up against President Godfrey in peak condition and win. If they did that, no one would complain."

"Exactly. Who wants these dull cowards 'olding sway over our lives, eh?" Rossi chimed in.

Then Andrews glanced up, receiving a message via the mana frequency from his flying familiars.

"Ms. Khiirgi sounded the retreat. We'll have to invent an excuse. We're done, Albright."

"One minute. Haven't yet crushed this shrew."

"Not so fast," said Ames. "I have a wild beast to dispatch."

"Go, go, Jaz!"

"The Jazinator!"

Albright and Ames were completely ignoring the spirit of things, entirely absorbed in their duel. Tim glanced at that—as Mistral healed his hand—and laughed.

"Least *you're* having fun. That's how Kimberly kids *should* be," said Mistral. "Still, pull out for now, Ames. I'll ref your fight with him later. You can go at it all you like once you're back on campus."

This proved enough to make both sheathe their blades. Watching them reluctantly back down, Tim thought: *If that's all it takes to stop them, this generation's a lot better behaved than mine.*

"Tch!"

"Eeeeek...!"

"KYOOOOOOOOOOOOOOOOOOOOO!"

Team Liebert had been circling on their brooms, dropping spells on the teams below—but now a griffin was hot on their heels. No one on their team was really a skilled flier, and they were ill-equipped to handle a beast built for aerial combat. Chela glanced up at that and smiled.

"...I see Lyla's here. Isn't Katie so nice?"

The perfect reinforcement. Katie's team might have been tasked with securing the escape route, but she'd also been poised to send her griffin out as needed. The ideal foil to Team Liebert's long-range-spell bombardment.

"...Without support from above, we're sunk..."

"Not yet...!"

And with their backup gone, Team Bowles would have to handle things on their own. Fay's charge and Stacy's and Chela's spells weren't making that easy. Their formation was a classic one vanguard, two rearguard, but since the two casters didn't hesitate to land spells dangerously close to Fay himself, his headlong charges never left him exposed. The strategy hinged on how tough his werewolf form was and the rock-solid trust that lay between them.

Team Bowles was being pushed back but grimly hanging on—and then hands clapped down upon their shoulders.

"Good effort. If the situation allowed it, I'd love to let you finish things...," Elise Cuvier said. She'd cut off her fight with the Sherwoods and regrouped with her juniors. "But I'm afraid that's not an option. It's time to retreat, children."

"Whuh?"

"We're still good to go!"

"I know you are, but this one dumbass dropped the ball elsewhere." Cuvier sighed. "There's no use pressing for results now. It's time we backed off and regrouped."

Bowles and Howell swore, and Chela lowered her athame.

"Then it stands as a tie," she said. "Perhaps not quite what we agreed on, but I shall share word of this anyway and tell people the true Team Bowles was formidable."

"...I love you, Ms. McFarlane...," Rodney whispered.

Their nerve-racking spell exchange had clearly worn him out. His team hopped on their brooms and flew away. Elsewhere, Team Liebert had also turned and fled.

Only when they were well and truly gone did Stacy lower her blade...

...and a new voice echoed over the momentary calm.

"Awww...I'm too late?"

They spun around and saw three figures riding on broomback. They came in for a landing some twenty yards away. Chela narrowed her eyes, appraising the new arrivals.

"...And who might you be?"

"Hiii, Ms. McFarlane! I don't think we've, like, talked much before?" The girl in the center stepped forward. The axis of her stride was unsteady, rocking back and forth. Each line she spoke rose in pitch at the end. Those traits rang a bell.

"You're in the finals, aren't you?" Stacy said. "Team Valois, I believe? Your friends have bailed already, but are you still game?"

"I wiiish! But we're under orders and stuff. So I'm just saying hello! We'll see each other in the finals, yeahhh?"

Ursule Valois let her head flop sideways, big, round eyes locked on Stacy. Chela and Fay both grew uneasy and stepped in front, hiding Stacy behind them.

"You're so, like, tight-knit," Valois said. "That's why I *despise* you guys. You and Team Horn and Team Andrews! Just watching you all makes me want to barf."

"Huh?"

"...?"

This one-sided revulsion just baffled them. Valois's eyes bore down on them, revealing no emotion. Her voice was equally flat.

"It's nothing *personal*, y'know? And I don't care about belc or dragrium, but, like, if I don't win, that'd kind of...suck? So I'm just gonna trounce you all. Let Team Horn know, yeah? Okaaay, we're done here."

She spun on her heel, hopped on her broom, and flew away with her teammates in tow.

"...What's *her* problem?" Stacy said. "She came all the way here just to say that?"

"Perhaps she was issuing a challenge before the finals. Her team remains an enigma," Chela replied, not having gleaned much from this brief interaction.

Stacy nodded and put it out of her mind, poking her servant's back. "Fay, you holding up?"

"Just getting nice and toasty," he said, as if he never got tired.

Shannon headed toward them, and Gwyn called out, "Rivermoore's undead are gathering. Keep your wits about you—the real fight has just begun."

"…Hnggg…!"

The kick Khiirgi had soaked sent her flying downward in a diagonal line but she managed to snag a branch of an undead plant with one hand—only to be hit with spells from Oliver's team below.

"Progressio!"

Cornered, a spell echoed from her lips, and the dead trees around her reached out, wrapping her in a sphere. An emergency escape at a high mana cost. The enhanced branches fended off follow-up blows, but within, Khiirgi was coughing up blood.

"Blegh…! Hurts every time you kick my guts in. I had an arm in between to soften it, but my ribs are still pulped!"

"I was trying to snap your spine. You want more?"

Lesedi landed on the sphere, stomping it. Khiirgi wiped the blood from her lips with a smirk.

"…Let's not. I mean, I'd love to keep going, but Leo would be furious. He might already have it in for me," she said. "Whatever! I managed a minimal delay, at least. Can't exactly bring everyone here for a full-on brawl. The rest is in Rivermoore's hands—I'll have to go home and let our adorable Percy chew my ear off."

"Glad to hear it. Mow this lawn first."

At that demand, Khiirgi shrugged and mouthed a chant. The magic circle fertilizing the undead plants lost power, and the vegetation quickly withered away. They had always been an entirely unnatural growth and could not survive long outside their highly specialized environment. When the collapse reached her, Khiirgi slipped out of the sphere and sped away on a broom.

Watching her go from below, Oliver asked, "...You sure we should let her?"

"No telling what'll pop out if she's in real trouble. And for once, she actually controlled herself. When she's being really vicious, it's far worse than this," Lesedi replied with a snort.

This was only a taste of the elf's true strength—a thought that went right past *shudder* into *cringe*.

Then a voice called Oliver's name.

"Noll!"

"Is everyone okay?"

His cousins and Team Cornwallis. They came in for a landing, and Mistral's teammates joined them and Oliver's squad. Lesedi quickly took control.

"More teams should be joining us shortly, but they'll have undead on their heels. Stick to the plan. We'll be splitting into offensive and defensive teams, but first, let's rework the squads a bit."

With that, she turned directly to Gwyn and Shannon.

"Sherwoods, I want you with Team Horn on the invasion crew. Wish I could go myself, but Khiirgi wore me out, and I'd better not fight Rivermoore like this. If you've got fuel left, take over."

"Can do." Gwyn nodded.

"Hee-hee-hee! We get to be together, Noll!"

Shannon happily put her arms around Oliver from behind. With them on board, Lesedi turned to the others.

"Then I'll take over supervision on Team Cornwallis. You'll be with me on defenses. I'm expecting good things."

"Hmph. I assumed I'd be on invasion."

"Stace, let's not fight this one," Chela urged. Stacy had her arms crossed, but her half sister had figured out the logic behind the assignments. "I doubt they'll be putting any other third-years on that team."

Lesedi nodded heavily. "McFarlane's ahead of me, but yeah, the invasion team'll be the three members of Team Horn, plus three upperclassmen. Soon as Tim gets here, I'll be having him join you to complete the squad. From here on out, one upperclassman won't be enough to mind three of you."

Balancing offense against defense, accounting for the situation at hand. If all other squads were here, maybe she'd have chosen differently, but the old council's disruptions would have most of them arriving too late. Since this plan hinged on speed, late arrivals would have to get put on defense.

Then Tim flew in with Mistral and Team Ames in tow.

"Sorry! Screwed up and got bogged down!"

"You're the last member," Lesedi spat. "Spare me the excuses—make it up inside."

With that, the invasion team was complete. They took a good look at one another, and Lesedi made the call.

"Our mission lies on your shoulders. We'll keep your escape route open—go get Godfrey's bone back!"

All six nodded. Nanao's entire body was positively aglow with ardor—and Yuri's eyes shone with a gleam every bit as bright.

"…They're in."

Naturally, Rivermoore was well aware of their movements. He'd been sharing his familiar's eyes, but he cut that loose and strode away.

"You're going out yourself, Cyrus?" the coffin called.

"The Sherwood siblings and the Toxic Gasser. Can't leave them to the ghouls. At least Hard Knocker's staying out…"

His voice sounded grim. He'd fought them all before and understood just how tough they could be. As did they—this was a fight between people who knew each other's bag of tricks all too well. That would not make things easy.

"We'll begin as soon as I've taken care of them. Be ready."

"Okay...and good luck."

Rivermoore rarely looked this tense, and Fau solemnly watched him go. She knew this would make or break things but felt no anxiety. He'd promised to return, and she could not imagine him breaking that vow.

They were headed belowground, so the first thing they had to do was secure an entry point. Since this was Rivermoore's domain, he could open a door with a single spell, but uninvited guests would need to force their way in. They'd laid out a magic circle and were watching the center bore its way down.

"...Shannon," Oliver said. "One thing before we go farther."

"? What is it, Noll?"

Shannon smiled at him, and he pulled a bone fragment out of his pocket, laying it on her palm. It was the fragment Yuri had been holding on to.

"We recovered this from the zahhak. I'd like to see the memories in it, if we can."

"Do we need to?" Tim said. "We're at his workshop! More clues won't do shit for—"

"I'm in! I wanna see!"

"Then so shall I!"

Yuri's and Nanao's voices drowned out Tim's doubts, and that made Gwyn chuckle.

"If they insist, let's take a look. Shannon, keep it quick."

"Mm. Okay."

Shannon held up the bone in her hand, closing her eyes. Silently, everyone placed their wands on hers.

He'd been in the workshop all morning, organizing a huge mound of bones. After a solid two hours of labor, something started bugging him.

"...?"

It was too quiet. She hadn't said a word this whole time. They'd talked a bit when he awoke that morning, but since then, his talkative friend had been laying low—and once that dawned on him, Rivermoore got up and moved over to her coffin.

"...Hey, what's with the silent treatment? You finally learn how to play dead?"

He rapped the coffin with his knuckles. Still no answer. He snorted, assuming she was just in a bad mood. He wondered why but decided he'd better work out first if she was angry or depressed. He leaned closer—

"Someone's pulling my arm, a ray of light, dark, cold, cold, cold, I don't want to be here anymore, I don't care if it's fire, I need light, give me back my shape, a form, a form, the smell of soil, the feel of the wind, I can't remember anything—"

"—!"

This torrent of words proved his notion had been terribly optimistic. He put both hands on the coffin, his face up against it.

"Fau, I'm right here!" he called, desperation in his tone. "Hear my voice! Don't let those thoughts drown you!"

The endless loop went still, and a feeble voice came back to him.

"Ah...ah...oh. C-Cyrus? W-was...was I...?"

"Yes, that's right. Talk to me, not yourself."

Grabbing the tail of sanity as it floated toward him, Rivermoore pulled as hard as he could, bringing her back to his side. Her voice quivered with confusion and fear, but her words had meaning once more.

"I—I had...a really scary dream. You were gone. I kept calling you, but you never answered. I waited, but you didn't come back. Th-that *was* a dream, right? This is real?"

"I'm right here. I'm not going anywhere, and I won't leave you. No matter what."

His vow came in a low, steady tone, and he repeated it again and again. Each time he said it, she was a little more like herself.

"Heh...heh-heh. I didn't know you could be this nice, Cyrus. Are you sure you're not a dream?"

"I could make it a nightmare. What if I painted your coffin pink?"

"Augh! That's it—this is real! I remember now! I'm a piggyback ghost riding you around. No point in going all groggy! I got work to do!"

She spoke with her usual cheer again and was back to mouthing off. But the chill in the pit of Rivermoore's belly remained. Until he'd pulled her back, she had very much been a step away from succumbing to the darkness permanently.

The relentless flow of time was like a spear prodding at his back. He'd always tackled his duty with urgency, but now he needed a huge leap forward, one that would make his prior efforts seem like a snail's pace.

He knew what to do. He made what preparations he could and went to see for himself—see what mages usually first encountered on their two hundredth birthday. For better or for worse, anyone who delved to the fourth layer of Kimberly's labyrinth earned that privilege.

"...Plans have changed. I don't *have* thirty years," Rivermoore said, athame in hand, facing a pitch-black shadow.

Every instinct in his body told him this was a terrible idea, but he forced those thoughts away, aiming his wand at the thing that had slain his great-grandfather.

"Show me how high this wall is. **Congreganta!**"

His memories grew fuzzy from there. How had he fought? How

had he escaped? Rivermoore himself was unsure. The next thing he knew, he was lying in a heap in the marsh on the third layer, in the throes of a crushing depression.

"Cyrus! Cyrus, are you okay?!"

When he dragged his aching bones back to his workshop, the coffin greeted him with a fretful cry. The channel between their ethers meant she already knew what had happened.

"...Relax. If this was fatal, I'd have died on the way here."

Rivermoore crumpled to the floor. He looked like he'd been through the wringer, but there were few external injuries. It wasn't his body that hurt—these wounds were in his ether. A state you'd never wind up in fighting a beast or another mage.

"Don't be insane! Even the dead's hearts can stop, you know! Why would you go fight one of those things?! You knew you stood no chance the second you first laid eyes on one!"

She sounded ready to cry. Catching his breath and enduring the pain from his ether, Rivermoore answered, "...The day of the old man's two-century passage. You remember what he asked me?"

"...? The thing about getting further? Of course I remember. You were so confident..."

"Yeah. Naturally, I meant it at the time. But thinking back, that answer was rehearsed. I said I could surpass him, but how much did I really believe that?"

"_____"

"Part of me knew he couldn't come back alive that night. I'm sure I don't have to tell you, but necromancers are ill-equipped to ward off death's embrace. Our skills are little more than a systemic list of tricks to skirt the rules of the world and keep the dead moving. No matter how much you advance the art of necromancy, it does you no good against death itself. I believe that's why, despite the long history of the Rivermoores, we've produced no long-lived mages."

"It's not like you to be this gloomy, Cyrus," the coffin's voice echoed, consciously choosing to remain upbeat. "One little loss got you down? Then let me promise you this. You're just depressed. One thing went wrong, and you're letting it get under your skin. Sleep on it, and you'll be right—"

"I can't afford to waste a night!"

His voice erupted over hers. Fau gasped. No matter how bad a mood he'd been in, no matter how many frustrations he'd faced, he'd never once let his emotions lash out like this before.

"Fau, give me your best guess. How long do you have?"

"——!"

"Every coffin but yours has gone bad. I'm sure Great-Grandpa knew it. Our duty would run out in my time," he told her. "Determining the means to banish that thing is the one way I have of surpassing the old man. But fighting one made it all too clear. It's not enough—neither my talent nor the time I have left."

Fau couldn't find the words to argue that conclusion. How could she? She was the one putting this time limit on him. But she'd read something else between his words.

"...Cyrus," she began. "Were you hoping to do *more* than your mission? Hoping to bring me back for good? Has that always been—?"

She heard his teeth grind. He knew he lacked the power, but still that wish smoldered within him.

"It's just not right. Why won't this world let that happen?"

The memory ended, leaving them blinking.

"...See?" Tim groused. "Just a bunch of shit we were better off not knowing."

"I thought it was very educational!" Yuri exclaimed. "It all makes sense now!"

Before them, the magic circle had finished its task. A hole bored ten feet through the center of the ground, a cavity yawning beneath.

"Ready, Noll?" Gwyn asked.

"Yeah. Let's do this, Brother."

Tim swept past them both, jumping in first. The others soon followed. They fell through darkness for a solid five seconds, then used a deceleration spell to land softly.

They glanced around and found themselves on a staircase descending still farther into the depths. The walls were covered in countless bones, human and magic beast, lit by the flickering glow of candles, their empty eye sockets staring back at the intruders.

"...Catacombs," Gwyn growled, clutching his athame. "A graveyard beneath the kingdom of the dead—sounds bizarre."

"Looks almost like a museum," Oliver said. "And an oddly quiet one. Doesn't feel horrifying."

The visuals were certainly striking, but he sensed no loathing or rage from the cadavers around. They had the same aimless emptiness as the undead above, although these had been properly placated and were resting quietly. Oliver was intruding upon their rest, and it made him wish to leave them undisturbed.

"Doesn't change what we're here to do. C'mon."

Tim led the way down the stairs. The Sherwoods smoothly took the rear, with Oliver, Nanao, and Yuri in between. For a while, the only sound was their footsteps.

After a minute's descent, they reached a set of doors, and rather sturdy-looking ones. Tim raised his blade to burst through—but before he could utter a spell, the doors opened on their own.

"Magnus Fragor!"

Open or not, Tim still fired a doublecant burst spell through. Flames and smoke belched out. Brushing those aside with a gust spell, the Toxic Gasser threw himself inside, the others on his heels.

"Mind your postures, grave robbers. Do you not know any visitation etiquette?"

Inside was a vast hall, with multiple ascending staircases as wide as the one they'd come down, placed side by side. The warlock's voice rang out from the top of the stairs, at the far end of the hall. Cyrus Rivermoore.

"Here already, Rivermoore? No undead welcome?"

"Wish I could have offered one, but I didn't want you spilling poison all over my workshop. So I decided to handle you here."

All six braced themselves, but the warlock snorted.

"I hate to ruin the enthusiasm, but this isn't a fight. You've come this far, so you have two choices."

The walls behind him began to tremble, and something vast and white burst through the stones: a jaw lined with teeth each as big as a man, twin horns like steeples, and sockets like pits into the bowels of hell. A sight so sinister, Oliver's skin broke out in goose bumps.

"...Is that...?!"

"A behemoth skull," Gwyn said. "He dug it up on the second layer a while back."

"That took me a while," Rivermoore said. "But it's the holy body of a divine beast. The soul's clinging stubbornly to it. Couldn't handle it as materials or a familiar, so I had to make it guard the place. Didn't think I'd ever need to use it."

The giant jaws yawned open, a sea of smog swirling within. Oliver gulped.

"You know what will happen here," Rivermoore continued. "It'll breathe on you. Being undead reversed the element, but it still has the power of the age of divinity. Do any of you know how to stop that?"

That breath could easily fill this room. There was no way to dodge, and even if all six joined forces to block it, it would tear through them like tissue paper. Tim swore. Aboveground, he would have had options, but down here, they were out of luck.

"Like I said: choices. Make yours. You can all die here, or you can drop your wands and surrender. And to be clear—retreat is *not* in the cards. If you take one step up those stairs, the breath will follow you. Your deaths will be all the worse."

"You son of a—"

"Tim!"

Gwyn stepped in, stifling the Toxic Gasser's rage. Tim gritted his teeth. It took him a long moment, but at last he hung his head.

"...I ain't dumb enough to miss when I'm beat. Fine! We're done. Out!"

Defeated, he dropped his athame. Rivermoore's brows twitched.

"How obedient. I thought you'd squirm a lot longer."

"Bitch, I've got kids with me. Can't go buck wild like I used to."

Tim flopped down on the floor, legs crossed, glaring up at their foe.

"If you'll allow me some sour grapes—you're a damn good student, Rivermoore. You're *still* watching my every move, and you've got the high ground and the wind at your back, perfect poison foils. You come at us with these unique techniques, but you've got the fundamentals down, too."

"I don't have time for this. All wands on the floor, white or metal."

Rivermoore clearly didn't believe Tim had actually surrendered. He wasn't letting his guard down until everyone was disarmed and unconscious—and well aware of that, Tim kept talking.

"That's why I already ended it. Or did you think I couldn't predict all *this*?"

That was when Rivermoore spotted several tiny creatures wriggling on the wall behind him.

"___!"

"""""""Impetus!"""""""

Before the warlock could react, the scorpions ruptured the cysts on their backs—and the squad below kicked up a gale *away* from Rivermoore. They'd been downwind from the get-go—this accelerated the existing wind flow, and the mist of scorpion poison threated to envelop the warlock above.

"Tch—!"

Escaping that forced him to leap to the fore. Tim snatched his athame, bounding to his feet and racing up the stairs with his team on his heels. Rivermoore dispatched the mist with a spell, but the gap between them was gone—he was now at the center of the stairs, surrounded.

"Yo, you sure you should be all the way down here?" Tim taunted. "Don't this mean your precious divine beast breath'll hit you, too?"

Avoiding the mist *had* put Rivermoore in range of the undead behemoth—and an attack here would take them all out together.

The scorpions were—of course—Tim's familiars. He'd expected a trap that took advantage of the close quarters and sent them around ahead of time before they came rushing in. He'd fired a burst spell through the open door to cover their advance, letting the scorpions scuttle around the outside walls and across the ceiling before the smoke cleared, sneaking up behind Rivermoore. There was a concealment effect on the familiars to keep them from being spotted on the way, but even then, Tim's performance had kept Rivermoore's attention on him.

With six athames pointed his way, Rivermoore sighed.

"…You just don't appreciate how nice I was being. You that desperate to turn this into a death match, rabid dog?"

"Damn straight. Was I unclear? I came here to kill your ass dead."

There was a vicious gleam in Tim's eyes—and every bone displayed on the walls sprang to life. Oliver gulped.

"Suit yourself, Toxic Gasser," the warlock said, grinning. "I'm all out of magnanimity. You and your poor juniors will rot away right here."

"Ha-ha! Bring it!"

Tim sounded downright delighted. As they stood poised to begin their dance of death—they heard a hiss. Something at the far end of the room was *melting*.

"——?!"

"Whoa, Mr. Linton, your poison's awesome! Even a sturdy door like that goes down in nothing flat!"

That tone didn't fit the scene. Yuri had gone off on his own and was standing below the behemoth's skull, where Rivermoore had first appeared. The door before him had collapsed in a puff of smoke, revealing the passage beyond.

"...Mr. Rivermoore," Oliver said. "You're a powerful foe. Especially on your home ground."

He was picking his words carefully. The battle hung in the balance, and Yuri had slipped out ahead—and those two factors offered them a third choice.

"But our goal here is not to defeat you. All we care about is recovering President Godfrey's bone. You know perfectly well we have no reason to stay and fight."

As he spoke, Yuri stepped through the door, waving back at them from the far side.

Rivermoore frowned. "...You believe you'll get anywhere groping around in the dark? My workshop is hardly that small. Can you find what you seek?"

"That, I don't know. But we're in a hurry, so our search will be rather reckless. Who knows what damage we'll do on the way. What if something that *matters* got hurt?"

Oliver let that line hang. The more a mage pursued singular magecraft, the more they stood to lose if their workshop got raided. Especially when preparing for a major ritual. It would be impossible to put that out of mind and focus on the fight at hand. That was why Lesedi had told them ahead of time—their target was not Rivermoore but what lay behind him.

"...Is that a threat?"

"No. I'm proposing a deal."

Refusing to wither in the face of the warlock's glower, Oliver got down to brass tacks. This was likely the sole route to ending this mess in any positive light.

"We'll be taking back President Godfrey's bone. But—*after* you've achieved your goal. We can wait until your ritual is complete. Our goals need not be opposed; both can be achieved to our mutual satisfaction. Correct?"

"Ha?!" Tim snarled, glaring at him.

"This meat has a mouth on him," Rivermoore growled. "You speak like you've deduced my intentions."

"You're resurrecting a coffin discovered here. And salvaging necromancy lost to time."

That certainly made Rivermoore waver.

"That's not a deduction. We *know*. We gathered the bone fragments from your undead, and my sister read your memories from them. Allow me to apologize for intruding on your past uninvited."

"...The Sherwood girl? Quite a stunt you had hidden up your sleeve."

He gave Shannon some side-eye, but then Yuri called out from the rear passage.

"Oliver! Let me say the rest. I've figured some things out after seeing the undead here. Mind playing along and seeing if I'm right, Mr. Rivermoore?"

"...I'm curious. Do go on," Rivermoore said, his back still mostly turned toward Yuri.

"The core of your magic is etheric bonding."

"_____!"

"The undead, by their nature, do not grow. You might get them to re-create what they knew in life, but once dead, they fundamentally can't learn new things. Yet, the undead you wield are full of surprises. Skelebeasts that reassemble themselves into new forms, wyverns fused with the dragoon riding them, zahhaks that bust out totally different skills in the middle of the fight—no way they could do any of that while alive. This whole time, I've been trying to figure out how you can even *do* that."

Yuri spoke eloquently, his voice rising and falling—almost like a song. Oliver could tell from listening: He was having *fun*. All peril forgotten, simply digging into the secrets of the Case of the Stolen Bones.

"And my answer: You've been joining etheric bodies. Stitching different ethers together, manufacturing new undead. Ether is closer to a being's true nature than the flesh ever will be, so if you can connect them up, alterations to the container are the easy part. To you, bones with ether affixed to them are like glue-covered wood."

"......"

"The key here is that it's bonding, not fusion. Pure speculation, but I bet if they meld into each other, it doesn't work. They'll lose their individuality, like the restless hordes do. The essence lies in connecting the undead to these etheric outlines, preserving the nature they had in life. That's why you put so much effort into managing the undead. To preserve the contours of their being, to prevent them forgetting who they were—that's why you re-created the fallen kingdom here."

Yuri broke off, swinging his athame in a circle. He wasn't casting any magic, so Oliver took this as a gesture born of heightened enthusiasm. Unspooling this mystery had him at peak excitement.

"Back to the point. Resurrecting this ghost requires a flesh equivalent to what she had in life. Naturally, there's no hope that her body would have survived the last thousand years. You have to make a new one from scratch, but obviously this can't be some slapdash puppet. If you need her to reproduce ancient necromancy, post-resurrection, she has to be capable of acting like a mage."

Yuri wasn't hesitating to break down the sorcery of a mage far beyond his capabilities. Oliver remembered the phrase *"curiosity killed the cat"* and shuddered. Even if Yuri had come here without a single ally, he would have done the exact same thing.

"That's why you've been stealing students' bones. Carefully, pains-takingly selected mage bones assembled into flesh worthy of the one you wish to revive. And the last piece you needed was President God-frey's bone. Which means—you're poised to attempt the resurrection ritual that's been the focus of your entire life."

Yuri brought things to a rousing close, and Rivermoore folded his arms.

"...Loath as I am to admit it, you're right on the money," he said. "But why the optimistic belief that Purgatory's bone will survive the ritual intact? Usage incurs degradation. At the least, alteration."

"But we have evidence to the contrary. The fragments of your bones we recovered from those undead have not been altered. Since Ms. Shannon could read the memories from them, that much is clear."

Yuri had clearly anticipated this question. Every scrap of infor-mation they'd acquired on the way in was a clue leading him to the solution.

"You're using ether as glue to hold the container's flesh together. With the resurrection, the techniques involved will be on a much higher level, but the principle is the same. It's easy enough to imagine that your bone fragments in those undead were that link and played a core role—if they survive intact, then there's no reason to assume President Godfrey's bone will be damaged, especially since it's just one of many. They're bound together, but not fused—and that suggests the process is reversible. Right, Oliver?"

Rattled by the pop quiz, Oliver thought for a second, then said, "I'm with Yuri. And I'd add that when we defeated the wyvern rider, we saw a portion of the creature still moving, severed from the whole. I assume that's because it was no longer in contact with your bone, and thus the connection to the ether was severed. That *also* suggests your etheric bonding is reversible."

Rivermoore's frown was deepening, and Oliver took that as a sign to press his advantage.

"Naturally, there's an element of risk. Our analysis is partly speculative, and it's possible the bone will be damaged for reasons even you can't anticipate. Even so—balanced against the losses both sides will incur if this fight continues, I'd say those risks are well worth taking. Wouldn't you, Mr. Rivermoore?"

Pressed for a commitment, Rivermoore's silence was weighty. His eyes left Oliver and turned to Tim, who still looked ready for murder.

"...Lesedi intentionally sent the Toxic Gasser in here to force me to the negotiating table. She always did have a knack for plays that could easily go very wrong but somehow don't."

Oliver privately agreed. Without Tim Linton's volatile nature, these talks would never have begun. Not just because his poison had opened the hole in the wall—but because his very presence here could well wreck the entire workshop, and Rivermoore could hardly overlook that. Lesedi's plan had hinged on taking his life's work hostage.

The next silence was even longer. His expression showed no dramatic changes, but there were clear signs of turmoil and strife. At long last, those faded away, and the warlock lowered his wand.

"................Fine. It is *hardly* what I intended, but I shall upgrade you from grave robbers to guests. In appreciation of your 'solution.'"

Despite Rivermoore's words, he looked ready to rip Yuri's head off. Yet, Yuri just grinned back, looking proud of himself. Rivermoore snorted and turned toward him.

"But you *will* mind your manners. This is a tomb. Respect the dead within."

Meanwhile, the turns at the front line had ripple effects on the defenses above.

"Hmm."

Lesedi's foot pulverized another ghoul, and she ground to a halt. A ripple of confusion ran through the crowd. The relentless army of undead attackers was now standing stock-still, like so many scarecrows.

"The fight's gone out of them. The invasion crew either beat Rivermoore or closed a deal. Either way, good for us."

"Do we join them?" Chela asked, eyeing the entrance.

Lesedi considered it, then shook her head.

"...No—if they've brokered a deal with him, rushing in could upend it. Be on standby, ready for anything."

She took a canteen from her satchel and quaffed the water within. All that fighting had her body overheated, and she needed to cool down.

"Looks like we're in the endgame," she whispered. "Unless something else flips the board."

They'd pulled off a delicate negotiation by the skin of their teeth, but that didn't mean the conflicts were over. Tim Linton had a lot of disgruntled griping left in him.

"...Yo, over here. The hell's going on? Nobody told me a damn thing about this."

"Sorry, Mr. Linton. Ms. Ingwe's orders," Oliver replied. "Said you'd be more intimidating if you had no clue a deal was in the cards—"

"I'll give her that. I was hell-bent on killing this son of a bitch. Now I gotta take all that fury and stifle it somehow. Just look at this poison I wasted!"

Tim jammed his elbow into Oliver's side, and Shannon put her arms on her cousin's shoulders, trying to pull him away from the needling.

"Enough goofing off," Gwyn said, at his limit. "No matter how we got here, we're now witnesses to the rite. Let's not disturb the minister's focus."

He jerked his chin at Rivermoore's back. They took any number of branches and moved through a door at the end of a passage into a reception room, with a coffee table set between two couches. Rivermoore waved a wand, and the crystal lamps filled the room with a warm glow.

"Sit where you please," he intoned. "I've never invited anyone living, so I can't vouch for the comfort."

"Some hospitality you got there," Tim spat. "At least offer tea."

"I never said I wasn't."

Tim flopped down on the couch. A door at the back opened as if in response to his snark, and a skeleton in butler clothes came in. It had a tray in both hands with six steaming cups of tea. As its guests gaped, it set them down at even intervals on the table.

"I've got a few checks to run before I start the ritual," Rivermoore said, not even turning to face them. "How long are you waiting for?"

"Max twenty-six hours. Given the run back to campus, Godfrey's recovery, and enough time to prep for the finals...we can't really go longer."

"That'll do."

Rivermoore vanished through a door in back. If this was going to be a while, Oliver would rather sit—except he wasn't entirely comfortable kicking back in the warlock's lair. But Nanao and Yuri didn't even hesitate. Worse, they reached for the tea.

"...Mm. Most excellent."

"?! You drank that, Nanao?!" Oliver said.

"Indeed. I sensed no ill intent."

"Mr. Butler, sir, can I get another? All that talking left me parched!"

Yuri sure had a lot of nerve, but the bone butler bowed and poured more tea from the pot. Oliver couldn't believe his eyes.

"Settle down, Horn," Tim said, holding his own cup out for more. "If there was poison in it, I'd know. I'll handle the whole vigilance thing, so you just unwind a bit. This had to have taken a lot outta you."

He was clearly speaking from experience. Yet, Oliver still hesitated. Only when Shannon pulled his arm did he finally sit down. The butler brought out cookies—to Nanao's and Yuri's evident delight.

Upon depositing his guests in the parlor, Rivermoore headed to the back of his workshop. He moved right to the waiting coffin and gingerly explained the situation.

"...Not how I planned it, but they weren't taking no for an answer."

"Ah-ha-ha-ha-ha-ha! This is a real turnup! I love it! The more the merrier! You've told me lots about your school friends, so I can't wait to see them!"

She sounded every bit as pleased as he wasn't. Having expected that, Rivermoore snorted and rapped his knuckles on the coffin.

"Final tuning on your flesh is done. The rest is down to focus. Prepare yourself."

"I'm ready as I'll ever be. I sure had enough time."

Her confident response was the push he needed. Rivermoore nodded and seated himself at the center of the magic circle next to the coffin. He took several long, deep breaths, quieting down the adrenaline of the fight, clearing his mind—so that his heart would not waver no matter what lay ahead.

Two hours after their arrival in the parlor, Oliver's lap had somehow become a pillow for both Nanao and Yuri.

"...Mmmph... See...they're tasty, Oliver..."

"......"

Yuri had gone down first and was talking in his sleep. Oliver heaved yet another sigh. He'd moved to this couch on the grounds that his sister's embrace would never end otherwise, only to wind up with these two all over him—and now he was trapped between them.

"Oliver, if I may venture a question…"

As he watched Shannon nod off on the couch across from him, a voice drifted from his lap. Nanao's eyes had opened, and she was looking up at him.

"Your discussion with Rivermoore was, from the start, based on the assumption that the bone would be returned."

"It was. We can't be entirely sure the bones won't be harmed in the process, but weighed against the risk of fighting—"

"That's the point that escaped me. Before any considerations of degradation, we are discussing the return of a departed soul from the afterlife. What is now a heap of bones will be granted flesh anew. And once that has happened, I cannot imagine asking for the bones' return."

Nanao folded her arms as she spoke—and Oliver at last spotted the source of her confusion.

"Okay, let's wind it back a bit. I see why you're lost now. My argument was based on a pretext you are unaware of. Let me get you up to speed."

He took a moment to martial his thoughts, to consider his approach. She'd been at Kimberly two years and change, yet there were still occasional discrepancies between Nanao's knowledge and those of your typical mage. Especially in areas unaffected by practical concerns. He was filling these gaps in when he stumbled across them—he rather enjoyed it, really.

"First, our world does not *allow* the dead to resurrect. This is not a concern of law or theory but the fundamental world order—one that invokes the frenetic principle. It violates the rules our 'god' made. This is something that no mage can escape as long as they are acting within *this* world."

"I had imagined as much. Yet, that is what Mr. Rivermoore aspires to."

"I'm getting to that. Second, Mr. Rivermoore's ultimate goal is the revitalization of ancient necromancy. Strictly speaking, this resurrection is simply a means to that end. When mages attempt a resurrection, that is nearly always the intent. What matters is not the return to life but what you stand to gain from it. Bear that in mind."

On his lap, Nanao nodded. Seeing that, he decided not to rush through this. They had plenty of time on their hands.

"Imagine an ancient scroll, exposed to the elements and badly deteriorated. You wish to unfurl it and read the contents, but touching it at all could make it crumble to dust. So you take every caution, utilize all means available to you, and attempt to decipher it. Mr. Rivermoore is doing this not with a scroll but with a human being," Oliver explained. "Resurrection is an extreme means of doing so, but in terms of our example, it's akin to transferring the entire contents of the scroll to a new piece of paper. Making a copy—in this case, moving the soul to a new body. And that counts as the resurrection the world forbids."

He paused there. To ensure she fully understood, he would have to dig a little deeper.

"Incidentally, there are other phenomena that might *appear* to violate this rule. Possession is an infamous example. In that case, a ghost will take over flesh that is not their own, but it's less a new host than something they've wrapped themselves around."

"Wrapped?"

"It's tough to explain, but…to put in terms you'd understand, let's go with horses. Horses are the flesh, and the rider is the soul. Only the horse's real rider—the genuine soul—can move that horse. A rider can dismount from their horse, but not climb onto another. Ghosts are riders who have lost their horse. Despite this, they want a new horse more than anything else—so they cling to a horse's torso or legs, trying to bend it to their will. That is how possession functions. Since that's just an analogy, there are several practical differences, but essentially, possession is an extremely unnatural and ineffective means of control."

"Mm, I'm with you so far."

"Since possession is so ineffective, it's not counted as resurrection and doesn't violate the world order. Necromancers take advantage of that, giving the dead temporary hosts and turning them into familiars. But in that form, only a portion of the soul's true power is available. They have no growth potential or creativity, and it's difficult to maintain high-level thought. You can make it so they perform basic tasks like the undead here, but if you need to bring someone back *as a mage*, that simply won't do. Most magic can only be performed if the caster is currently alive."

Nanao closed her eyes, murmuring thoughtfully. Oliver went over things once more in review.

"Let me summarize. Rivermoore wants to revive ancient necromancy, but to do that, he has to fully resurrect an ancient mage. Unfortunately, the rules of our world forbid that. You with me there?"

"I believe my understanding suffices."

"Then let's get to the real point. If you must violate the world order and perform a resurrection, there are theoretically two primary approaches. One is to head to a different world and perform the resurrection there. What is not permitted in our world may be allowed in a world governed by a different god. But this is a pie-in-the-sky idea— one purely theoretical."

"Oh? Whatever for?"

"None of the tírs that mages are capable of reaching allow resurrection the way we'd want it. Compare it to the laws of nations—theft is illegal in Yamatsu and equally here in Yelgland. Same difference. There are any number of other practical concerns—but for now, assume resurrection in a tír is impossible."

Nanao nodded. There was plenty more to discuss about tír themselves, but that was a tangent best left unexplored here. He'd have to fill her in some other time.

"Which means Mr. Rivermoore has only one path remaining.

Namely, he must create his own world in which to attempt the resurrection."

"...You mean..."

Nanao looked tense. Knowing exactly what she'd pictured, Oliver nodded.

"You've been to one: the sights we witnessed during Ophelia's incident. The Grand Aria—that technique allows a mage to deploy a domain that operates under different rules, turning infringement legitimate. Resurrection included. If the Aria is designed to allow that from the get-go, then nothing there can prevent the resurrection. Out of all possibilities, that is the one place Mr. Rivermoore's purpose can be fulfilled."

If the world did not allow it, then make your own world. That was perhaps the highest expression of a mage's craft and every bit as difficult as it sounded. Not something that could ever be achieved in a single generation.

"...Even if a mage of exceptional talent prepares very, very carefully, it's nigh impossible to keep the Aria under control. Just as we saw with Ophelia, if you surpass your limit, you'll be consumed by the spell. Which means anyone resurrected within will survive only until that limit is reached."

Nanao's eyes filled with understanding and a deep sadness. She knew the harsh truth, and Oliver consoled her, stroking her hair.

"Mr. Rivermoore's manner made it clear. We're about to see both the resurrection of a mage—and her funeral. We'll stand in silent vigil until the task is done. And when all the dust settles, we'll pluck one bone from the remains and take it home."

A good eleven hours after they were brought in, Rivermoore finally called for them. The bone butler led the group down silent corridors to the ritual chamber, where a coffin was placed at the center and a magic circle covered the entire floor around it. The space itself was considerably larger than any previous rooms. Oliver could tell this was the undead kingdom's throne room.

"...Before we begin, I want to make one thing clear," Rivermoore said.

He stood before the coffin, speaking softly. No signs of the heightened emotions he'd displayed in their earlier battle. His mana itself was tranquil, yet brimming over the edge. His focus was clearly honed—and it made everyone present instinctively straighten up.

"During the ritual, no matter what happens, you are not to intervene. You are witnesses only. In return, I can guarantee your safety."

"Naturally, none of us is foolish enough to meddle with a ritual we can't possibly understand," Gwyn said. "I swear we will remain seated even if you perish before our very eyes."

Rivermoore nodded once and turned to the coffin. Neither side belabored the point. They could easily disrupt the ritual if they wanted, but in that case, Rivermoore would destroy Godfrey's bone. If either wished to achieve their ends, they would have to keep their hands to themselves.

The moment was upon them. White wand in hand, Rivermoore slowly turned around.

"*Hahhhhhh...*"

One last deep breath, and before their watchful eyes—his chant began.

Omnes suas calvarias ad eandem partem vertentes ceciderunt.
Corpses on the ground, their gazes aligned.

A shiver ran down each spine. Oliver felt an urge to flee rising up within and did his very best to force it to subside. He'd been too preoccupied to observe the last Aria, but this time was different.

Hi ipsi pedes quibus feriebant terram hae ipsae manus quibus serpebant ad punctum temporis mortis eorum.

Their feet had tramped earth, their hands had clawed the dirt—until the end arrived.

Yuri's cheeks were flushed red. Nanao's lips screwed up tight. Even without prior knowledge, any mage knew on instinct alone—this here was the summit of Rivermoore's sorcery.

Ossa dissipata clamant se ipsos etiam egere et feriendi et serpendi.
Your weathered bones cry out for further tramping, further clawing.

Dum voces vestrae sonant nemo vestrum mortuos est.
As long as those voices cry for more, none of you are truly dead.

Rivermoore's wand pointed at the ceiling, and something began encroaching on their surroundings from below. Innumerable black threads, winding around one another as they ascended. The air above their heads was dyed a uniform shade.

Tectum sericis nigreas novum caelum hoc ipsum non ad vos ascendendum sed ad abscondendum et tergendum est.
A veil of black silk, a canopy betwixt you and heaven, obscures your path to ascension.

Sub caelo nigro nullus mortuos sed est vivens sine sanguine et carne.
Beneath that inky sky, there are no dead, only living souls lacking flesh.

As the canopy closed above, all colors, all sense of distance were lost. The world was shrouded in darkness. Shannon clenched Oliver's hand.

Dulce dormitatione vetita morte iucunda deposita ergo electa est vita doloris.
Death is rejecting the temptation of slumber, abandoning peace and tranquility; we choose the suffering that is life.

＊   ＊   ＊

The invocation droned on. The total darkness was broken by warm lights, emerging one after another.

Neque sanguis neque os neque caro sed ipsa voluntas est signum vivendi.
Life lies not in the flow of blood or the flesh itself but in the will alone.

A world born, its range beyond spatial magic, the mage's will manifest, a new order imposed by one man. Infringement made legitimate.

Sub hoc nullum sepulcrum est. Dum animas vestras tu reveritis vivitote in aeternum.
There are no graves here. You shall live until your very soul has frayed to nothing.
"Mundus sine morte–Paradise Lost!"

No moon or stars. Yet, the night sky above was aglow with a dim light.

Countless undead wavered indistinctly, passing back and forth overhead. Perhaps they were no longer undead. In this domain, the loss of flesh no longer signified death. If they had the will to choose suffering, then their beings remained on *this* side of the line.

"…Whoa…"

Oliver was left stunned. Every single thing in sight had been repainted, now far more pastoral than he'd imagined. At the end of his gaze, Rivermoore was wiping the sweat from his brow.

"Don't confuse me with a mad genius like Salvadori. My great-grandfather developed this Aria. I merely inherited it."

With that self-deprecation, Rivermoore turned his eyes from the view above back to his coffin. A Grand Aria was the peak of any mage's labors, but today it was merely setting the scene. His true designs lay on what was to come.

"I'm popping the lid, Fau. **Patentibus!**"

Rivermoore swung his wand wide. The sound of countless locks opening echoed—and then the lid slid aside. Outside air rushed into a bed sealed off for a thousand years.

"**Spiritus animae resuscitatio!**"

And the spirit within—left alone, it would likely soon disperse, but Rivermoore swiftly led it to the flesh nearby: the body of a young girl, assembled from bones gathered over the years. He could *feel* a new interior taking over that host.

There was a long silence. The body remained at Rivermoore's feet, not moving.

"Hmm—"

"C'mon, you can't blow it here!" Tim called.

Unable to directly observe the movements of the soul, all they could see was the shimmer in the air—but their concerns proved unfounded. Rivermoore waved his wand a third time.

"She needs a wake-up call. **Tonitrus!**"

A bolt from the tip of his wand struck the body in the chest, forcing the heart to start beating, the blood to rush through the body once more. The pale face regained its color.

"Owwwwwwwwwwwwwwwwww!"

Her eyes snapped open, and a howl escaped her throat—from silence to full throttle, but Rivermoore just stood and watched. She rolled around at his feet for several seconds, clearly in agony; then she got her hands on the ground and stopped. A few more seconds passed, and her head went up—tears in her eyes.

"...Why?! Cyrus, why lightning?! All this time I've waited, and you give me the worst awakening possible!"

"Don't blame me. You took too long to kick-start your heart."

"There are other ways to resuscitate people! At least try some healing first! And whoa, your voice! *That's* what it sounds like in person?! Do it again! Let me hear it one more time!"

The girl scrambled, running over to him. She stretched way up to reach his face, poking his cheeks with her fingers like a baby does with their parents' faces. She was delighting in the capacity for touch.

"...You look so *old*, Cyrus. Aren't you twenty-two? What happened?"

"Dealing with the dead takes its toll on you. You're more or less what I assumed. I know you're excited, but how's the body working for you?"

Letting her touch all she wanted, Rivermoore started checking her over. His question made her gasp and look at herself. She hopped up and down a few times.

"...It's *incredible*! What? How—? This might be better than when I was alive!"

"Good," he said, nodding. "Well worth the time I spent on component selection."

She tried reaching for his face again, but then she remembered he was not alone. She spun around to face the others, beaming at them.

"You're Cyrus's school chums, right? Nice to meet you! I'm Fau. I'm an old-timey mage who stubbornly refused to pass on. Thanks for attending my second coming!"

"...Sorry," Tim said. "I get that she's saying hi, but no clue what language that is."

To the group's ears, it was a stream of unfamiliar sounds. As the other five members blinked, Gwyn put his chin on one hand, listening close. It was rare he expressed this keen an interest.

"The language of the ancients," he noted. "In hindsight, not surprising. How would an undead learn Yelglish? We understood her in the memories because it was filtered through Rivermoore's perceptions."

"So I have to interpret?" Rivermoore said. "You've just woken up, and you're already a handful."

Fau and the others could communicate only through him. The next few moments were all regular chatter; the two had almost forgotten why they were here. With her ever-changing expressions and good cheer—she certainly acted the age she appeared to be. And that made this even harder for Oliver. She was too young for the burden she bore.

"My mind and senses are working fine," she noted. "So what about mana?"

Fau drew the wand at her hip and held it aloft. A flame appeared at the tip, and she began to dance—the choreography distinctive, to say the least. As she moved, the wand's tip kept changing colors, and each time it looped, the pace of her steps quickened.

"…!"

"Oh-ho! Such elegance."

Oliver's eyes went wide while Nanao let out a cry of delight. Attribute shifting at a high tempo was a magical warm-up Oliver himself employed, but when Fau switched elements, the transitions were nigh invisible. That alone proved she was a deft hand at mana manipulation, but what really boggled the mind was how smoothly the mana flowed through her entire body. Attribute shifts inevitably sent ripples through you, but Fau's were barely noticeable. Training your flesh for mana use alone wouldn't do that. This control lay deeper, likely within the ether itself.

Once she'd danced her fill, Fau came to a graceful stop and spun to face Rivermoore.

"Mm, all good. Then let's get started, Cyrus. I hate to rush, but…"

Rivermoore nodded. "Right. Come on in."

He turned away, heading to a little hut on a hill inside the Grand Aria. The witnesses, gathering that the necromancy instruction would take place there, silently watched them go. Fau followed Rivermoore, turning back once to wave. Oliver couldn't help but grin. She was so easy to like, it was hard to believe she hailed from a millennium ago.

"Nn—!"

But Rivermoore stopped in his tracks just outside the hut. Fau looked up in surprise, only to sense the same thing a moment later. They both spun around, staring back the way they'd come—and soon *everyone* knew what was wrong.

"Something's coming," Yuri whispered, staring up at the void. A crack appeared in empty space.

"...That's...not good..."

As the world crumbled, a pale bone arm thrust through, clad in black rags. Fau winced, and Rivermoore turned pale. Both knew all too well what this was—and what it meant for them.

"...The Aria seal was incomplete. They've caught our scent."

With no legs to stand upon, a black cloth hovered in the air, only the arms and a scythe emerging. The blade itself reflected no light, existing solely to end lives. All here knew the bearer. Innumerable songs, poems, and children's tales told of its grim visage. Rules established by the fallen god brought an end to all life in kind.

The second law of the frenetic principles: No one lives forever.

"A reaper...!"

The name crossed Oliver's lips like a shudder. As he stood rooted to the spot, Rivermoore and Fau drew their wands.

"Resuscitatio!"

In answer to their chant, twelve figures rose from the ground. Ancient mages of all genders and ages. Zahhaks Rivermoore had long made use of, reborn as the living here within the Grand Aria. The passage of time may have worn away their personalities, but the spell correctly rebound their flesh and souls, allowing them the use of spells and dramatically heightening their combat potential. The last card Rivermoore had up his sleeve.

A hitherto unseen skelebeast rose up from the feet of one ancient. Another deployed a shadow, from which emerged a massive bulk. Still a third was surrounded by a swirling vortex of curse energy. No time for analysis—every attack was launched directly at their quarry.

And like so much wheat, all were mown down by a single swing of the reaper's scythe.

"——!"

Thus began the promenade of death. The skelebeasts were pulverized, and the reaper's ire turned to the ancients themselves. The first put out a bone beast to shield itself—and the swing cut through both as one. A second dove into its shadow, attempting to flee, but the scythe sliced through shadow and diver. The spectacle was overwhelming, and Oliver's every bone rattled. The ancients threw all their long-lost secrets at it as one, and it was not even a *contest*.

"Gah…!"

Rivermoore clenched his teeth. Within the Aria, loss of flesh held little meaning, but the reaper's blows sliced directly to the ether itself—and with that damage, resurrection was not possible, even here. Less than a minute after the fight began, his final hand of cards had been reduced to half their number.

And still the reaper rampaged, bearing a message from the world on death's inevitability.

"…No use," Tim muttered, watching Rivermoore and Fau struggling in vain. "Given that only one reaper showed up, the Aria greatly diminished their power…but necromancers just don't have what it takes to fight a reaper."

"————"

Even as he spoke, Nanao unconsciously reached for the blade at her hip, unable to bear it. But Tim clapped a hand on her shoulder, his grip firmer than ever before.

"Don't even *think* about helping them. This thing's only after the resurrected girl—and Rivermoore, because he's protecting her. As long as we don't stick our noses in, the reaper won't bother us."

"Hrm."

"This is why Rivermoore made us swear not to intervene. This ain't a matter of logic anyway. You can feel it on your skin!"

Tim raised his hand, showing it to the third-years. Oliver gulped. Tim Linton, the Toxic Gasser himself, the Watch's crazed berserker, a mage who'd faced down death countless times—and his hand was shaking.

"Even if the president was with us in peak condition, I wouldn't wanna fight that thing. Two-hundred-year-old mages are absolute monsters, but eighty percent of them fall when they first face the reaper. That's how powerful this curse is. You don't stand a chance against a thing like that, not with underclassmen in tow."

This was patently obvious, and all the more convincing since it came from Tim's lips. As a grim silence settled, Gwyn added his two cents.

"I'm afraid Tim's right. Even if they go down, we've still got a shot at recovering Godfrey's bone. And that's our best bet."

The only real option left to them here: watch the reaper mercilessly cut Fau down, then pluck the bone from her corpse and beat a hasty retreat. They had no idea if Godfrey's ether would remain intact, but they'd just have to cross their fingers.

"........."

Putting a tight lid on his emotions, Oliver ordered himself to remain still. This was for the best. No matter the outcome, they could not afford to lose anyone on this team. Rivermoore had been their enemy not long before, and Fau was on his side. No matter how you looked at it, this was not worth risking all six of their lives.

"Gah...!"

"Cyrus, step back!"

A blow from the reaper had damaged Rivermoore's ether, and his face contorted in pain. Fau stepped forward to guard him, but Rivermoore himself pushed her back, adamant.

His heart frozen, Oliver realized: By the tenets of all mages, the Scavenger's actions were in error. Unable to fend off the reaper himself, Rivermoore's ritual had already failed. There was no point in fighting. If you considered the future ahead of him, then the right choice here would be to let the reaper claim Fau. All Rivermoore was doing was putting his own life at risk for nothing—and he likely knew it.

"...Honestly. You *would* do that," Fau said with a laugh.

She'd already turned her wand to her own chest. *Ah*—Oliver felt a sigh echo through his heart. He knew only too well how she felt and what had led her to that choice. He'd have done the same himself in her shoes.

A short breath followed. Then a spell echoed across the night sky.

"...Huh?"

Her wand braced, Fau gaped, forgetting what she'd been poised to do.

Before her, the reaper had *stopped*. A bolt of lightning had come in from the side just as it was about to attack Rivermoore again. Its scythe held high, the agent of death's very being momentarily fluttered like a candle in the wind.

Fau and Rivermoore both turned to see who'd done the deed. Sparks still fading around his athame, well out ahead of the observer's post, a boy stood—doing the most foolish thing possible.

"Noll..."

"Hah?! The hell are you *doing*?!"

Shannon's eyes were on her little brother's back, and Tim's face turned another color.

Rivermoore had never dreamed of this intrusion; he glared at Oliver like a wounded beast.

"...What's the meaning of this, third-year? I told you not—"

"It's not for *you*!" Oliver roared, the words ripping out of his throat. He was all too aware how inexcusable this act was. This was not for Rivermoore, and deep down he knew it was not for Fau, either.

He had no compulsion to overturn the principle of human death. That would be a rebellion against the design of life itself and was entirely separate from his own heart's desire. And yet—the sight

unfolding before him was *not* acceptable. Snipping this girl's life by
the same standards applied to mages at the end of an already extraor-
dinarily long life—the pigheaded nature of that rule filled him with
such fury, he felt positively dizzy.

Glaring at the reaper, Oliver asked: *Where is the* sin *in this
resurrection?*

This girl had endured eons in a lightless casket, solely for the purpose of passing on her knowledge to the future. Time she should have
spent out in the sun had been whiled away, buried in darkness. She
had waited there, grappling with the terror of her very self withering
away. All for a fleeting resolution that might never come to pass. The
significance of her birth entirely depending on it.

To her way of life, he felt equal parts sympathy and respect. But
those were not what moved his hand.

When the man who brought her back was in danger, Fau had not
hesitated to end her own life, well aware that doing so would invali-
date all the time she had endured within that coffin.

Rivermoore had fought a reaper twice. Once now and once some
time before. The first time, he'd hoped to grant her new life; the second, to ensure the life she had was not in vain.

Oliver wished only to guard those urges. Even if that was stupid,
even if that was the wrong choice, he *had* to do it. He fought to protect
not the ritual, not the secrets of ancient necromancy, but their hearts.
The kindness of a boy and girl, unbroken by the harsh toll of time's
passage.

*Hear me, Grim Reaper. I do not ask you to leave this place, only to
bide your time.*

"…Complete your duty, Cyrus Rivermoore! Though the world may
not approve! That's what we mages *do*!"

A shout from his very soul, directed at a mage far more powerful
than Oliver. Rivermoore stood as if struck by lightning—and then two
figures joined Oliver.

"Pray, what is the plan?" Nanao asked, drawing her katana.

"Uh, how do we fight reapers again?" Yuri asked, his head cocked askew. "I mean, they don't die."

Oliver forced aside the urge to apologize, deeming that best not said here.

"Nanao, Leik—"

"Only one way to handle these things. Hit 'em with effective elements, continuously canceling the phenomenon. *Never* get hit; their swings strike only ether."

Gwyn and Shannon flanked the trio. Oliver's expression momentarily crumpled.

"Brother, Sister…"

"We know…what you want to do, Noll." Shannon raised her white wand.

"Doesn't matter what we're up against. If your heart desires it— then we are here with you." Gwyn shouldered his viola, and the sole remaining upperclassman pushed his way between Oliver and Nanao.

"You're all a bunch of idiots. Lesedi and her dumbass schemes… She really blew it this time."

"Mr. Linton—!" Oliver gaped at him.

Tim drew the athame at his hip and cast Oliver a sidelong glare. "And here I thought you were *less* crazy than we were. Boy, was I ever wrong. You've gone and jumped right into madness here."

The Toxic Gasser clicked his tongue. Thorough preparations, situational advantage, fighting only foes you knew you could beat—Lesedi had talked her mouth off going over those principles, and they were the ironclad rules of the Campus Watch. But all the older members knew—they'd broken every one of those rules countless times in their day.

Their foes had never once seemed beatable. Opponents they had to fight, enemies they had to beat—those had never arrived at their convenience. If they had time to calculate their odds, they'd be better off casting another spell. If they had someone worth protecting, then they'd wade into the fray with that alone in mind. And the crucible of those gambles was their source of pride.

This was no different. In other words: It was merely Watch tradition.

"Fine! I'm in. Didn't know what else to do with these vials anyway. But lemme just say this—if any of you dies here, I'm kicking your ass myself."

His very mana laced with bloodlust, the Toxic Gasser bared his fangs. The reaper recovered from its stunned state and began moving.

"Twenty minutes, Rivermoore!" Gwyn yelled. "We'll keep the reaper at bay till then! Can you make the most of it?"

The warlock clenched his jaw, then grabbed Fau's hand and turned to go. No time to hesitate. He had a purpose to fulfill.

"...I owe you!" he called.

Those were words he'd not used once since his start at Kimberly. Running by his side, the corner of her eye on the six fighters behind them, Fau smiled.

"See, Cyrus? You have *lots* of friends!"

That provoked the dourest expression human flesh was capable of making. But before anyone caught a glimpse of it, Rivermoore and Fau dove into the hut on the hill.

Yuri made sure they were in, then said, "I think I solved another mystery, Oliver."

"?"

"The Case of the Kindhearted Friend. I've always wondered: Why do you worry so much about other people? It'd be so much easier if you just let them be, no matter who was risking their neck or where."

This left Oliver rather rattled, to say the least. But Yuri spoke with conviction.

"I finally figured out why. You value the heart most of all."

Oliver staggered as if shot through the chest. But Nanao tugged at his sleeve.

"I knew that much already," she said.

"No time to flirt! It's here!" Tim roared, vial in hand.

They braced for battle—and the reaper swung its scythe.

Inside the hut, Rivermoore put a seal on the door that would hardly last long, then caught his breath, glancing around. There was a big, round worktable at the room's center; a dozen varieties of powdered magingredients in little dishes; and a row of mummified fetal corpses. All were children who had perished in the womb—and like Carmen had heard, he'd acquired these from mages' homes. He breathed easily. Everything they needed was here.

"...No time, so let's skip ahead."

"You got it," Fau said, nodding. "Overlap your space with mine."

She moved to the worktable, raised her white wand, and went still. Rivermoore joined her, using spatial magic to merge his perceptions with hers. Ears and eyes alone would not suffice here.

"...*Hahhhhh...*"

Eyes closed, she let out a long breath—and *something* the eyes could not detect rose up from the fetal cadavers. Fau wound that around her wand like so much taffy, then cast a spell that made the amorphous *thing* separate into layers of disparate density, arcing before Fau like a rainbow. Imperceptible to the naked eye, Rivermoore could only perceive it within his personal space.

"...!"

"Soak in the feel of it. You're pretty good at etheric bonding but still at a patchwork level. To reach the next stage, you'll need to make finer divisions in the ether, applying clear measurements to it. Like cutting wood in regulation lengths. It's a lot easier to work with than the whole log, and there's so much more you can make from it."

As she spoke, Fau's wand kept moving. Like peeling bark, the rainbow's layers came apart from the outside in, lining up in the air. Rivermoore was blown away. He, too, had been working on ways to split and classify ether, but the most he'd achieved was three layers. Meanwhile, the rainbow Fau was peeling apart was divided into seventeen. That alone showed the sheer discrepancy in their respective necromancy.

"Naturally, this is easier said than done. Etheric research lags behind research on the flesh for the simple reason that it is that much harder to observe. As a rule, you can neither see nor touch an etheric body. Even ghosts who flicker like a candle in the wind—what you're actually seeing is the air, dust, and magic particles moving as the ether passes by."

Each word Fau said, each move she made—Rivermoore was heightening all his senses, trying not to miss a thing. This was what she'd been born to do.

"Almost the only exception is here, within a mage's spatial magic. In that space, what we perceive lies outside the five senses, and some people are able to directly perceive and manipulate the ether there. Problem is, that's highly dependent on the individual's background and impossible to make universal. Anything that takes place in a mage's personal space is inherently subjective. You can tell someone an apple is red, but no words can truly define what being red entails. Same logic."

Even with the spaces overlapped, facing the same subject, what Fau and Rivermoore sensed was *not* alike. Sensations within personal spaces were far more disparate than those experienced via the eyes and ears, organs of similar construction. At best, that was a nursery that could raise a mage of singular sensibilities, but at worst, it could create an impassible information-processing incompatibility. Since these sensations were yours and yours alone, there was no way to communicate them to others.

"Since we *are* both mages, we've got ways and means of sharing experience vicariously. But it's ultimately still a game of whispers. The information exchanged is fundamentally altered by the senses of the recipient, and the more people it passes through, the more significant the alteration becomes. This is hardly specific to necromancy; it's the reason mages create heirs with similar sensibilities, allowing them to pass down their techniques with minimal deterioration. But that simply elevates a personal skill to a family heirloom. Great if you want it kept secret, but useless for making things widely accessible."

As Fau talked, the powders on the table before her wafted upward, mingling with some of the etheric layers. Once she'd used the full amount of all twelve components, Fau began merging the layers back together again. The disassembly and alteration phases complete, she was now demonstrating how to reassemble.

"Given the aforementioned issues, we ancient mages spent a long time seeking one thing: an etheric body all could see and touch in the same way. Only with that manifest could a measure of objectivity be applied to etheric manipulation; only then could necromancy go from being a household craft to an academic discipline. And we achieved just that—shortly before the collapse."

Rivermoore swallowed hard, and Fau raised her wand, quite literally bestowing life upon her creation.

"**Spiritus animae resuscitatio!**"

Wind and light in tow, her mana swirled. And within, a new creation let out its birthing cry.

Mere mortals up against death incarnate—Oliver was learning just what that meant with every fiber of his being.

First, he could discern no consistencies in its movements. The reaper just slid through the air above the ground, no feet to have footwork, the existence of footholds irrelevant. Yet, neither did it follow the principles of flighted creatures like brooms or wyverns; no experience with them applied here.

"*Tonitrus!*"

When it appeared to slow, he took aim, firing a lightning bolt at what he assumed to be its back. But the next instant proved all his expectations wrong. The reaper's body scattered like mist.

"____?!"

The black particles flew higher. No one was sure how to respond. The particles quickly spread out, turning into a large black cloud.

Gaping up at this, Yuri muttered, "Oh, it's gonna *fall*."

"To me!" Shannon called.

The others rushed to her side, forming a tight circle, and raised their wands overhead.

*""""""***Impetus!***"""""""*

Together, they deployed a barrier of wind just as the rain of death began. The drops dissolved the ground around them. The barrier was hardly immune to this, and only with all six pouring mana into it was it able to withstand the corrosion. Oliver gulped. If they'd been hit while separated, not all of them could have lasted it out.

"Do *not* assume a reaper has a set form! Death is everywhere and can be anything!"

Oliver chiseled his brother's warning into his heart. The rainfall ceased, and the mist rose up from the ground, gathering in the air above—and coalescing into a giant sphere. When it shot toward them, they scattered in all directions.

"Ah, it's gonna burst!" Yuri yelped.

"____!"

Everyone took another leap backward, and an instant later, the sphere imploded. Using wind to deflect the particles that flew his way, Oliver felt a chill run down his spine. If they'd gone from the first dodge to a counterattack, that could have ended poorly. But more importantly—

"Leik, can you read its movements?!"

"Yep! Seems like I know what it's about to do. I can hear it way clearer than those undead!"

Yuri appeared confident, and that itself was astonishing, but then Oliver realized—this was *because* they were fighting an avatar of death. The undead had been under a mage's control, while the reapers were a part of the natural order. He'd known Yuri's powers worked better with natural objects, and this foe fell right in line with that.

"Excellent!" Nanao cried, slashing aside reaper spray. "Then we shall follow your command!"

With that, she charged straight ahead. The fight so far had told her instinctively that they *needed* a front line. If they all feared incurable attacks and kept their distance, the reaper would simply shift shapes and come for them. But if, instead, they closed in, it would likely stick to its initial form and swing that scythe. Both options were a threat, but keeping it locked to a single form was preferable to the unknown.

"Ah, crap! Back off, Nanao!"

"Mm!"

As she neared its range, Yuri caught its next move and called her off. As they watched, the reaper grew highly condensed, exuding an uncanny pull. It was less a black sphere than a *hole* dug into space itself.

Feeling himself being dragged toward it, Oliver yelled, "Wind? No—this is curse energy gravitation! It's sucking us in!"

Spotting the nature of the attack, Oliver followed that with a pull spell at Nanao's back. She'd been closest to the reaper, and this dragged her to him just before the gravitational pull grew fatal. Each fought off the pull in their own way, standing their ground. From the moment of their birth, all creatures were equally affected by death's curse. The reaper was tugging the strings of that connection to drag them in.

"I've been waiting for this!"

But some mages could turn this to an advantage. Tim grinned viciously, and several things flew out from under his skirt. Winged insect familiars, the sacs on the abdomens filled with magical brews. Rather than fight the gravity, they flew right into the reaper's side, bursting. The fluid released was all inhaled as well, and the reaper's entire body warped. Steam shot out, and it started boiling in midair.

"A deluge of elixir! Suck on that!" the Toxic Gasser crowed.

Made by means only he knew, this was extremely concentrated and would prove highly poisonous if any human ingested it. Since the root concoction enhanced life functions, this same brew provoked a virulent reaction in a manifestation of death. He'd brought this along to handle undead threats.

Watching the reaper fade out in a puff of volatile white smoke, Nanao gave an astonished yelp.

"Is it defeated?" she asked.

"Don't be stupid," Tim spat. "If it were that easy, I wouldn't have been losing my damn mind."

True to his word, a familiar black form seeped back into view in the empty air a short distance away.

"You can put out a fire, but it ain't dead. You can scatter a breeze, but the wind won't die. No matter how many times you push it back, death ain't ever really gone. No matter how we fight this thing, we can't win—we're creatures with a finite life span, and that's what we get."

"Then we will just prolong our lives with all our might," Gwyn said and began playing his viola.

Surprised, Tim blinked. "A consolation concert? Does that work on reapers?"

"It's arguably the primary purpose. Death originated as a primal curse placed upon us by our god. Offering up the sounds of music is an ancient means of placating and distancing it."

And the proof lay before them. The reaper was re-forming as they watched, but the speed of that manifestation grew markedly slower the moment the performance began.

"Still...," Gwyn said, playing on. "We've already incurred its wrath. The best I can do is delay the inevitable."

"That's more than enough, Brother," Oliver said, blotting his brow with one sleeve. "It gives us time to recover."

Even a handful of seconds was worth a thousand gold.

Bathed in orange light, it bobbed in the air, vaguely humanoid. Rivermoore watched it with bated breath—as did Fau, its creator.

"...That's not..."

"Right, not a ghost," Fau said. "The etheric bodies I took from the unborn babies' ghosts formed the base, and I merged those with other ether and matter, reconstructing them into a man-made being. An astral life."

Fau let that name hang in the air. The astral life hovering above the workbench floated over to Rivermoore. Then it draped itself across his neck and shoulders, like a scarf with a mind of its own.

"It likes you already." Fau grinned. "Maybe because some of my own ether is mixed in?"

"......"

The astral life was staring intently up at Rivermoore, and he back at it. It showed no fear or caution—in that sense, it felt like a human infant.

"There's two fundamental differences from ghosts," Fau began. "First, like I said, anyone can see and touch it. The movements of the etheric body have been shrouded in mystery and subjective perception, but anyone can make observations with this little one."

Fau reached up and tickled the astral on the neck. It seemed to enjoy that. Clinging to Rivermoore, the astral life's lights fluctuated.

"And the second difference—unlike ghosts, this one's mind won't fade away, won't give way to hatred. Quite the opposite—it will learn and grow. It's as stable as our own etheric bodies, despite the lack of flesh. The components of its body are both material and etheric, those qualities combined. It is a complete life-form."

"…So not immortal."

"Right. Astrals can be lost by any number of means, and its soul is human, taken from one of these unborn babies. It has the same two-hundred-year limit we do."

Fau smiled sadly, then turned to Rivermoore.

"I know this child will be an invaluable research subject for you and all the mages of this generation. But if possible, I hope you'll look after it. As if it was *our* child."

"That's not something to joke about. But if it's going to serve my research for any length of time, I'll have to take good care of its mental health, too. No need to worry about that."

His tone was resolutely curt yet as earnest as Rivermoore was capable of being. He nodded, and the tension drained out of Fau's body.

"Okay. Then…then my work really is done."

Rivermoore's silence was weighty. He tried offering some words of comfort, but his throat was frozen and would not move. If he voiced agreement, if he thanked her—then it would all be over.

And she knew that. So she cut to the chase in his place.

"Sorry, Cyrus," Fau said. "Can I leave the last task to you?"

"Hyahhhhhhh!"

A bold step forward ducking under the scythe's swing, and with a roar, Nanao swung her blade up. All six mages battled the reaper in a state of extreme tension; release was a luxury they could not afford.

"*Hahhh, hahhh…* I—I can tell what it'll do, but…my body can't keep up!" Yuri gasped, stepping in as Nanao stepped out and pulling the reaper's attention to him.

Making full use of Yuri's predictive talents, he, Nanao, Oliver, and Tim were trading turns in the front line, minimizing the reaper's shape-shifting—that alone had kept them going this long. There had been several close calls, but Gwyn's and Shannon's precision assists had pulled them through.

"...Ngh...!"

But Oliver could feel their limit coming up fast. This style was especially taking a toll on Yuri, and Oliver swore to pull him out before it was too late, shouldering that risk himself.

"Hrm?!"

Yet, Nanao felt the threat on her very skin and spun around. All five others followed her gaze, spotting the same sight. Another black stain seeping into this space. The same threat they'd barely been handling before.

"...You're kidding! Now there's *two*?!"

Tim scowled. Reaper appearances had strict rules. When a mage reached two hundred, one reaper would appear each night. Every fifty years they lived, that number went up by one. Fau's circumstances were unusual, but if her age included all the years spent in the coffin before her resurrection, then it stood to reason there'd be more than one. Even if that wasn't the case, should other mages step in to help, the reaper quantity increased proportionally.

They'd had to deal with only one reaper because Rivermoore's Grand Aria had kept them at bay, but they had always known a second might make it through. Yet, knowing it was possible had not stopped them from hoping it wouldn't. And now that it had, they were at the end of the line.

"Ah—!"

Between his fatigue and the distraction of the second reaper, Yuri's step was a moment too late. The first reaper's scythe swung his way, and he knew too well he couldn't dodge or defend in time.

"Yuri!"

Oliver lunged toward him. He'd been right there watching, and only he could get there in time. He shoved Yuri out of the scythe's path, but that just made the reaper target *him*. The backswing was mercilessly coming his way.

"Sorry I'm late."

The blade stopped an inch from his throat. A girl's voice echoed across the land of death.

Six mages and two reapers all turned toward her. The hut on the hill—and Fau standing outside, the warlock a step behind.

"Thanks, Cyrus's school chums. Honestly, I didn't think we'd get *this* much time. I speak for all the Parsu people, in honor of your strength and spirit."

She plucked the corners of her skirt and curtsied. Both reapers shot toward her as one. The others were little more than an impediment; Fau alone had been their true target. She smiled at their approach.

"You two are *so* mad at me. Given your task, you would be. But don't worry. I'll make no more trouble."

Fau spread her arms wide, accepting the fate she had so long denied.

"I've done my part. The long struggles of the dead end here."

And with those words, Rivermoore's athame pierced her heart from behind.

The group gasped, watching over her. Fau's heart beat its last. The reapers bearing down stopped halfway up the hill—and as if the fight had never existed at all, they vanished without a trace. They no longer had any reason to be there.

"Ah—!"

For the first time, Fau saw the view around her. So preoccupied with her task and the urgency of it, she'd never even looked. Only now did she realize—they stood on an island, floating in the sea at night.

"Oh," she said. "This is a beach!"

The blade in her heart was retracted. Fau crumpled into Rivermoore's arms, and the astral life squirmed around them both, like a child fussing over its parents.

In Rivermoore's embrace, she used the last strength in her dying arms to point.

"Cyrus, over there. Take me there."

"Mm."

Rivermoore nodded, and a bone serpent rose up from his feet, carrying them both on its back across the ground past the crowd of witnesses, down the gentle slope to the little strip of sand at the water's edge. No moon hung above but there was a mystic glow, striking enough to evoke a little sigh from Fau.

"Wow, you've even got shells! Hee-hee. Gently lapping waves... How lovely."

"You made me take enough walks on the shore."

Cradling the girl, he stepped onto the sand, his voice wistful. Nothing he could do would bring her back for good. He could never take her to the real ocean's edge. And when that sank in, he'd made his choice. To at least show her the sea here.

Time passed quietly. There was only the lapping of the surf. Fau's lids slowly drifted shut.

"Thank you, Cyrus," she whispered. "You kept...your word..."

With the last breath she was allowed, she voiced her thanks—and passed away.

The world crumbled. The night sky shattered like glass, swallowed by the sea. Soon it reached the island the others stood upon. Ripples of white light covered their eyes, causing them to squint—and before they knew it, they were back in that cold stone room. Still sitting where they'd been when the ritual began. The man had his back to them, cradling a heap of bones.

"Mr. Rivermoore...," Oliver said.

"Take it."

He tossed something over his shoulder. Oliver caught it and looked down to find a human bone. Rivermoore had made adjustments to it for the ritual, but Oliver knew it was Godfrey's sternum.

"If you've got that, the doctor can patch him up. I won't forget the debt you're owed. So—it's time you all left."

Rivermoore never turned their way.

His goal achieved, Tim urged his juniors toward the door. As the others turned to go, Oliver took a step after them, then—

"If—!"

He stopped, calling out. Words failed him. But his mind caught a scrap of a memory, and he spoke as a witness to what had transpired here.

"...If she smiled at the end, then you have nothing to regret."

Oliver's voice never wavered. And with that, he left the grave behind. Rivermoore said not a word, letting it all wash over him.

END

Afterword

Hello. This is Bokuto Uno.

A mission from the dawn of time has been achieved, and the battle in the kingdom of the dead has concluded.

The warlock's scavenging achieved results—a strange form of life, a half step outside the world's order. Granted this by an ancient mage who dodged death's agents, how will it affect the present world?

The boy and his companions have met their goal, and their fight returns to the campus above. The foes waiting for them will be far worse than the previous matches. In every year, those still in the fight are the best of the best.

And yet, on this adventure, our detective learns much. Without him ever realizing it, his actions lead to the truth from the least expected direction. What sights will he see when he reaches his destination?

A major turning point in the third year indeed. But do not let your guard down. The passion of the league and the struggle in the shadows below—they have only just begun.

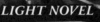

The DetECtiVe Is AlreaDY Dead

When the story begins without its hero

Kimihiko Kimizuka has always been a magnet for trouble and intrigue. For as long as he can remember, he's been stumbling across murder scenes or receiving mysterious attache cases to transport. When he met Siesta, a brilliant detective fighting a secret war against an organization of pseudohumans, he couldn't resist the call to become her assistant and join her on an epic journey across the world.

...Until a year ago, that is. Now he's returned to a relatively normal and tepid life, knowing the adventure must be over. After all, the detective is already dead.

Volume 1 available wherever books are sold!